THE BOTTOM OF THE RIVER

BY:

JASON TERHUNE

DEDICATED TO

"ANDY LANGIN"

R.I.P.

TOKYO DONG

"THE BOTTOM OF THE RIVER"

JASON TERHUNE

"INTRO"

Where the fuck am I? I am in a daze; I have been trying to shake it off but to no avail. To be honest I am not quite sure how long I have even been here; let alone where the hell here even is. I don't feel right, I'm groggy. I have that feeling going on, that one has when waking up after taking far too much Nyquil. You all know the feeling that bit of haziness and confusion.

I can see that the room is barely lit as my vision slowly comes back to me bit by bit. The

2

place looks like an old log cabin or an old shack. The whole place looks to be covered in that nineteen sixties style wood paneling, God I hate that shit. That old wood paneling was, hell still is the crap that covers the walls at my Grandmother's house in Pender. The floors are all wood but in terrible shape. I can feel with my toes that the wood is all ruff and grooved, covered in decade's old dust that long ago became part of the wood itself. Another big question wracking my brain at this very moment is why the hell am I barefoot?

There is a TV playing in the corner of the single room cabin. There is some fucked up channel on, the reception keeps going in and out. There is no volume on the TV at all, just that messed up picture going in and out. Now that I look a little closer it looks like it may be Bob Ross painting his happy little trees. It could be the news for all I know, the picture is weird and fuzzy, still flickering in and out. I'm a bit scared looking at the TV. I am reminded of that movie Poltergeist. I am hoping, hell praying that no Carol Anne shit is about to go down. I'm still groggy but things are beginning to be in far better focus. Now I am starting to feel like either this is a bad dream or I may be in a Saw movie.

My hands are tied. I can feel the rope against my wrist. The rope is thick, not the type of shit that they sell at Wal-Mart. No, this feels like the type of rope that cowboys use for their tricks, or the type of rope they used to make nooses out of and hang people with. You know what I am talking about, those types of ropes from a western or a horror film where someone hangs themselves committing suicide with. The rope isn't really all that tight. I can feel gaps in the knot with my fingers. That is one of the things about these old thick ropes, hard to get them tied all that tight.

My eyes have adjusted to the darkness now. I can see shadows over in the corner. The ringing in my ears that had been there is now gone. I can see a dimly lit lamp in the corner with at least five men huddled around it. I can hear muffled screams, as if someone has a hand over their mouth or possibly a rag stuffed in their mouth. Don't ask me how I know what someone screaming while having a rag stuffed in their mouth sounds like. I am alert now, yet I am smart enough to pretend not to be. I know that if whoever it is that has me tied up right now knows that I am fully awake well, I fear that the worst will come to me.

I can hear a slapping sound along with cheering. I peer through the shadows and see what looks to be a girl tied to a table and a boy who I wouldn't guess to be more than thirteen years old raping her. The other guys are all cheering the boy on. I want to look away, yet this whole scene is like a car wreck and I just can't pull my eyes from what's going on in front of me. What the hell is going on is all I can think? I can hear the four men cheering on the boy, as if he were playing football or something.

I can see all of their faces in the shadows now. They all look like hillbillies or rednecks to me. None of them look very clean or as if they kept up on their personal hygiene. Three of the four have half ass Joe Dirt looking beards. The only thing that is missing is Real Tree Camo and some old country music. There is a reason other than this live sex show going on right now that I am studying all of these guys. The odds are one hundred percent that I will be fighting these men, I need to size them all up.

I look at the girl, she is blonde, maybe five foot four. She has a pretty petite build, she looks so damn familiar. I know that I have seen her before, but where? Her face is coming into better view. I can see the tears running down her cheeks as the boy rapes her. I have no clue if this girl was ever innocent with regards to the evils of this world, sadly I know she will never will be again after this moment. No woman deserves this to be done to her, to be

violated like this. To be gang raped by a pack
of hillbillies or whatever the fuck they are.
This is Nebraska, these fuckers are probably a
group of fucked off tweakers, yeah that is where
I would put my money on, tweakers.

As soon as the boy is done the next sick
fuck begins to take his turn on the poor girl.
The fucker is pushing in and out of the girl
with no mercy. I feel for her, I feel her pain,
yet whatever I feel for her is over shadowed by
the fear of what is to become of me. I have seen
Pulp Fiction, and I have also seen Deliverance.
I assure you that I have no want or desire to
squeal like a pig, nor do I have a pretty mouth.
This being the case like I said, any feelings
that I have for this poor girl being gang raped
right now are overrode by my own fears. This is
fucked up to say but I am going to say it

anyway. I am happy that it is her up there right now. First and foremost that means that it isn't me up there. Secondly, they are all far more interested in their current gang bang fantasy right now than they are with me. Hey fuck it, she is one hell of a distraction.

The yokel finishes with a load moan as he fills the poor girl with his inbred demon seed. All I can think of right now is if I can get free I will kill all of these fucks, somehow some way dammit. I am also pretty sure with there being five of them and one of me I will be on the losing end. No, fuck what dad always said, "Go down swinging like a man", no strategy is the key to survival right now. I still have no clue how I ended up in this damn situation, it will come back to me. I can tell that I was drugged, good shit to. I take a deep breath in

as silently as I can and try to think. I have
done every drug on this earth, every drug just
to forget, to stop all of the nightmares, if
only for a night. This felt like a pill high, a
high that was wearing off, good for me, bad for
the hillbillies.

They untie the girl and take her off of the
table. I close my eyes and pretend to still be
out. I had been working my fingers between the
gaps in the ropes, they were loose now. I could
easily slip free if I chose to, I just need to
find the most opportune moment. They drag the
poor girl over next to me and throw her down on
the floor. I can hear her muffled cries, feel
the heat from her tears in the air. I can feel
the pounding of their feet through the floor
boards as they drag her over next to me. I hear
one of the guys call out

"Hurry the fuck up, get this bitch hooked up."

I am still pretending to be out, my heart is pounding so hard I am afraid it will give my rouse away. The poor girl is kicking, even kicking me. It takes everything I have not to move.

"What about this fucker."

I hear one of the hillbillies say while laughing.

"Oh he is next."

"Once he is awake we will play with him"

One of the men says.

"Give him a few hours and he will wake up, I hit him with two darts. Now get this bitch dressed out, it's already fucking noon."

Noon, now I have a reference for time, good.

"I want her dressed and ready for dinner tonight you got it Jimmy?"

The voice calls out.

"Jimmy since this is your first you get the honors of dressing her and getting her ready."

I hear a different voice say along with what sounds like a pat on the shoulder.

"Now remember Jimmy this is no different than dressing anything else okay"

"You be careful not to have to much more fun boy."

Another voice calls out laughing.

"No problem guys thank you for finally allowing me to be part of the family business. I promise that I won't disappoint you guys."

The boy's voice calls out. Sick fucks I think to myself.

I hear all of the men leave the room, leaving only the boy.

"Don't worry baby this won't hurt at all."

I hear the boy say to the girl.

"Don't worry I am going to give you this shot, you won't feel a thing."

The boy said to the girl. I open my eyes just barely and see the boy shooting something via syringe into the girl's neck. I can smell it, it smells like Everclear whiskey. I peak out of the corner of my eyes to see the girl passing out. I know her now, she is the girl from Wayne East truck stop. She is tied up, the boy pulls on her ropes flipping her upside down her arms and head hanging over a large gray metal wash bucket. I open both eyes just in time to see the boy slash the girl's throat with a butcher's knife.

The blood began to pour from her body, really spray like water from a broken hose. I have used this technique on animals that I have butchered before. You shoot them up with whiskey to knock them out, let them go to a warm happy place if you will. It is far better for the taste of the meat. Then once they are out cold you hang them upside down and slash their throat. This in turn will induce a heart attack which will purge all of the blood from the body in record speed. This technique cleans the meat and gets rid of any sort of game like flavor. The fact that this technique every Midwestern man has used on deer or hogs is being used on a

human makes sense to me, but that alone is so
fucked up to me at the same time.

The boy is one hundred percent engulfed in
his work. Slowly the boy puts his knife into her
belly and begins to field dress the girl that
the group had just been raping twenty minutes
before. I am aware, I am clear, the haze in my
mind is gone. It is now or never have I decided.
I slip my hands free of the ropes that had bound
me. The boy has already finished gutting the
poor girl. I look over to see him eating a piece
of the butchered girl's raw liver. Jill that was
her name, Jill from Wayne East. I steady myself,
the boy has placed the knife on the table,
totally unaware of the fact that I am awake and
free.

I leap up and begin pounding on the boy
like a mad man with all of my might, knocking
him to the floor. I can feel his flesh give way
with each blow, feel his bones break. He looks
at me scared and surprised as I pounce on him. I
grab the little sick fuck and drag him to the
table that poor Jill had just been tied up to
while she was being raped. The boy's body is
near limp after so many blows to his head. I tie
the boy up as quickly as I can. I then shove a
dirty rag from the floor into the boy's mouth to
muffle his screams just in case any of the other
guys are outside. The boy begins to come to as I
am looking down upon him. I walk over to the
table next to Jill's body and I grab the very
knife that he had used to gut and field dress my
friend.

"Hey boy did you enjoy that, did you enjoy
raping my fucking friend Jill?"

I remember everything now, my mind is clear,
I am fully aware.

"What the hell is the matter with you fucked
up people?"

The boy is trying to struggle, trying to
scream, his screams muffled by the rag that I
placed in his mouth. I want to laugh yet I
almost feel sad as the boy begins crying from
fear.

"I would take the rag from your mouth boy
but I know you would scream and we can't have
that. Boy you have me at a cross roads here, I
should go get help, call the cops, that is
what's right, the right thing to do, what I am
supposed to do. Yet, you raped and killed my

friend not to mention drugging and kidnapping me. Boy I don't know how many times you have done this to people before, but this time you got the wrong one."

I laughed.

"Young man in the immortal word of good old Doc Holiday, I am not your huckleberry. I do thank you for drugging Jill before you killed her though. I know why you did it and I know it was not out of kindness, but I am glad you did it none the same. I will pretend in my head that you did it to be humane in your own fucked up way. Here is your problem though boy, I am not humane, and everything I am going to do to you is going to hurt, it is going to hurt you very bad."

I laughed out loud at my own remarks. I pulled the boys pants down and off of his body, I could still see Jill's juices along with the rest of these sick fucks all over his cock and balls. I grab the boys cock and balls with my full force grip, the boy let out a muffled scream through his filthy rag stuffed in his mouth. Looking down on the boy directly into his eyes I smile as I take his own knife and begin to cut his cock and balls free of his body. The knife is good and sharp, I don't even have to use a sawing motion, the blade cuts like butter. The boy's blood begins spraying from the place on his body where his cock and balls used to be. I pull the filthy rag from the boy's mouth and stuff his cock and balls all the way down the back of his throat.

"Fucking rapist."

I say as I push the blade down into the boy's throat. Like I said the knife is sharp, real sharp. I am able to push all the way down cutting right through the spinal cord. I hear the spinal cord crack as I slice through it, severing the boys head from his body. I hold the boys head up in the air by his greasy hair looking at it, the cock and balls still stuffed into the boys mouth, blood running down the chin covering the start of a scraggly looking mustache. I take some of the rope that I was using to tie the body down and tied it to the boy's hair and hang the head from the ceiling. A little present for the rest of these fuckers when they return. I remember everything now, so what do you say that we start at the beginning?

"Chapter 1"

The day started out normal, it was like any other, well as I remember it anyway. It is hard to say just what exactly I actually do remember these days, what's real or what's imagined. Most of the time everything in my world can be a bit of a blur at best. Far too often I'm left wondering if I am ever alive or if I even exist? I am caught between two worlds really. I hate to admit this, but I have been a raging drunk these days. Now don't go off and try to say it is because of this or that, or that I am weak or any of that bullshit. I will be real with you, it has just been really hard for me to put some shit in my head straight. There comes a point in every man's life that he has to put shit

straight in his mind, you know get shit in order
if you will.

The average man out there has shit like, oh
I fucked around on my wife with some slut. That
or some shit like they stole some money or wrote
bad checks, petty ass shit. I remember one time
while looking down the barrel of a gun pointed
at me, facing my own death. A lot of shit went
through my mind in what seemed like ions but
really was just seconds. You would think that I
would have seen some deep philosophical shit,
but it didn't. Shit went through my head like
missing an old cat that had died when I was a
child named Gizmo, or if my mother had ever
known that when I was nine I stole ten dollars
from her purse. I even thought about an old
girlfriend that had given me crabs back in high
school. There was no deep philosophical

messages, no answers to the meaning of life, nothing like that. Real talk, I was rather disappointed.

I heard a loud bang, I knew it was a gun shot. I found myself laying in a pool of my own blood. Three of the men whom I considered the closest friends I had lay beside me dying as well. My whole body felt, well like a giant Charlie horse, only after the painful part. You know the part I am talking about, that crazy tingling feeling. I couldn't move at all, I couldn't see, all I could do was hear a loud humming sound, so loud that it was near deafening. I felt as if my head would explode from the sound alone. I thought to myself, fuck here I am I can't move, I can't see, I am not in any pain and I am pretty sure that I am hearing the sound of God damn creation right now. There

is no other option, I must be dead, God damn it
I am fucking dead! I lay there expecting the
Devil himself to come and retrieve me. I had no
doubt that I owed him a debt or two.

I was taken back to my childhood, my first
totally fucked up experience. You know how they
say that life has those defining moments? In
each and every one of our lives there will be
those moments that we choose to take either one
path or another. I was twelve years old when I
had my first defining moment. I will say that
until that moment I was innocent, or as innocent
as a young boy can be. Growing up in my home
innocents was lost at a very young age I guess
you could say. To the point though, how I lost
my innocents and how my life changed forever.

Logan Creek, a dirty nasty creek filled with farm chemicals and the run off from countless hog lots and cattle yards. Logan Creek as dirty as it is really represents every creek in North East Nebraska. Logan Creek sits just on the edge of town, good old Wayne, Nebraska or Wayne America if you believe the water tower. Just at the edge of town under the bridge leaving town heading south was a place in the creek that we all called the falls. Now don't get excited the falls were nothing big in the grand scheme of things. No the falls were simply a small water fall maybe six to eight feet tall that developed under the bridge. This small waterfall made a pool at their base that was maybe ten to fifteen feet at its deepest point and maybe twenty feet across. The water was dark, a mess of topsoil and the silt that made up the muddy bottom of the creek floor. The top of the water was a mix of bubbles caused by the chemicals being stirred up in the water. All Logan Creek was really is just a channel cut through the Nebraska countryside, as old as the land itself.

Mostly we all fished there, not that it would have been safe to eat the fish at all. Looking back I am still surprised that we didn't catch old Blinky, the three eyed fish from the Simpsons in that damn creek. I was fascinated with diving at that time in my life. Like all boys with crazy ideas mine was that I wanted to be a scuba diver or possibly a Navy Seal one day. Yet I was in Nebraska so it is safe to say that I had no beach to practice my new found interest at. With this sad sense of injustice being my reality all I was left with was that damn muddy old creek. This being the case I found myself at the pool next to the falls with my face mask, a snorkel, and a flash light. Normally I may see a catfish or two, maybe a turtle. I got lucky a few times and found some cool old bikes I am sure that some High School kids had stolen and thrown into the creek. I even found a dirt bike once yet had no way to pull it up from the bottom of the pool.

That day I went down to the falls armed with my face mask, snorkel, and an old Rambo style survival knife tied to my wrist in case I dropped it. I also had a can of spray paint hidden in my back pack so I could do a bit of graffiti under the bridge. Normally I would have my coat hanger fishing pole and a can of corn for bait as well to do a bit of chub fishing. That day was different though, I was on a time

limit and had to leave around noon to go cut my
grandma's lawn.

I put my mask on and my snorkel and made my
way into the water like I had so many times
before. The water was pretty clear that day,
clear and cold. It had rained up north so we had
a lot of cold run off that we wouldn't have
normally. I decided to go into the deepest part
of the pool. The rumor was that a couple of high
school kids had ditched some stole bikes in
there. I figured if I could find them I could
part them out. That day my head was filled with
the hopes of new five star mag wheels for my
bike.

I took as deep a breath as I could and dove
straight down to the bottom of the pool. I had
been practicing holding my breath for months now

and could go without air for almost three minutes. With my flashlight in front of me my mind was filled with hopes of finding a Diamond Back, or a Predator bike. Sadly for me this would not be the case that day. I saw something on the bottom of the pool that looked as if it were almost waving at me, moving with the current. I won't lie it scared the hell out of me when I first saw it. All I could think was maybe it was Swamp Thing or some other creature. With all of the chemicals in this water who knew if a monster could be born, some mutated animal or some sort of aquatic Big Foot. Yet I was undeterred and swam on and with all of the bravery as well as stupidity of a young boy I swam up to the object, my flashlight lighting my way. As I swam up close to the object I was terrified, there before me was the naked body of a dead man. I nearly shit myself, I kicked so hard for the surface that when I breached the water I must have looked like one of those submarines breaching the waves from the oceans depths on the Discovery Channel.

I got to the bank so fast that you would have thought that I was Jesus running on water. As I sat there on the bank catching my breath I realized that I had no clue what the hell to do. I found myself thinking what if this were no accident at all, what if this was a murder? I thought that if it was a murder and I went to the police who ever did it would come kill me for snitching to the pigs. Yet if it were just some poor fool who drown and got stuck to a log I would be a hero of sorts. All I could do is think that this situation could go either way.

I sacked up and grew some balls and decided to go back in the water. I was terrified, yet I had to see, I had to know. I swam down to the body and shined my light on the poor soul. Right away, I could plainly see what was an obvious bullet hole in right in the middle of the forehead of the dead man. I swam back to the surface long enough to catch my breath and then went back under the water. I shined my light on the dead man's feet, they were both chained to two cement blocks. As I looked over the poor soul one more time I could see that the fish had already began to devour his remains. I kicked my feet and swam back up to the surface. I quickly made my way to shore, loaded up my back pack with my gear and headed for home off to cut my grandmas lawn.

I never said a word about what I had found that day. Three months later some kids pulled up some remains while fishing. This is a bit crazy sounding but this is the first time I have ever told anyone about that day. I guess that I always felt that I would be in danger if I had. I was just a scared kid, in all honesty maybe I should have told the police. When they pulled the body up it was too far gone to be identified, just bits and pieces really. They never did find the head at all. Maybe if I had told the pigs the man could have been identified. Then again maybe it was the police who killed him? Either way if the dead man had any family they would have gotten some sort of closure. I don't know, I try not to think about it, yet I do now and again, usually when I least expect it. That day changed my life forever.

That was the day that I learned that murder was real, not just something that one watched on the movies. I learned that murder could even happen in Wayne, Nebraska. Twenty five years have passed since I found that man on the bottom of the river, to this day it still haunts me.

"Chapter 2"

    I am not quite sure why I even told you that story. I have kept it hidden so deep inside, I guess that I just had to let it out, had to finally tell someone. To the point it had nothing to do with what happened earlier in the day. I do apologize I tend to go off on a tangent or rant now and again. That is one of the problems, side effects, whatever you want to call it that comes with drinking to damn much. You get lost in your own mind now and again, you forget shit, the future, the present, the past all kind of blur together. That is one of the reasons that I drink really. I am not a social drinker, I am in it for one reason and one reason and that is to get totally obliterated, straight fucked up. The day started like any other day, right? I had been hanging out down at Wayne East with Jill, Wayne East is our local truck stop. I liked Jill, she was a cool ass chick. Jill and I were what people would call friends, well friends with benefits, whatever you want to call it, I have never really been one for labels. Even better than Jill giving me pussy, Jill gave me free booze. Jill always had a decent amount of good drugs as well. Adderall to get up, Xanax to chill out, every pain pill known to man, meth, and always good ass weed.

Jill and I snorted some Adderall in the back office, as well as her giving me some bomb ass head. I was excited Jill had written off two bottles of Honey Jack saying that they had gotten broken. Our plan was to go road tripping after she got off of work. For those of you not from Nebraska road tripping is a local past time. Road tripping consist of driving out in the country, drinking, listening to music, and most often fucking. Now I am not saying that this is a safe past time at all, but in Nebraska it is just something that we do. If you are a guy you know that if you go road tripping with a woman and bring some booze, you will get laid, inspiration enough right there to throw safety to the wayside.

I waited for hours for Jill to get off of work. I didn't mind though I just went to a buddy of mines place and had some beers and smoked a couple of joints. This is one of the few joys of Wayne, there is always someone to have a few drinks with and to get high with. I am pretty sure that half of this town has some sort of substance abuse problem. By the time Jill picked me up I was already pretty high and had a decent buzz going on. I couldn't count the times that Jill and I went out road tripping, same thing we did at least twice a week.

Jill and I headed out of town driving north past Wayne State College. I remember my days going to that college, seems like it was in another life time now. Damn I was so young, just a bright eyed eighteen year old boy. I remember old crazy Kate, so damn bat shit crazy, yet so was I. In a way we were perfect for each other. Our relationship was so damn toxic it was bound to fail. How many times had we cheated on each other, hating and loving each other at the same damn time? Back then we were all that each other had. I am glad that we both decided to move on when we did, it was a good thing for both of us. I close my eyes for a second and I can see her face once again, that and that juicy ass she had. I hope that her life is going well, I honestly do. I heard that she lives in Lincoln now, has a family and has vowed never to return to Wayne again, I can't blame her, poor girl had it ruff, real ruff.

Wayne begins to look small in the mirror as Jill and I head north towards Dixon and Concord. I guess Wayne is small, there are only maybe six thousand people living there when college is not in session. Just a small Nebraska town that if it were not for the college or possibly Chicken Days no one would ever hear about. In a way one could say that about nearly every small Nebraska town. Now I am not just going to put Nebraska towns in this category, every state has their small towns, Wayne, Nebraska is just what I know. For better or worse Wayne, Nebraska is my home, always has been, always will be.

Jill and I drove the gravel roads like two people on a mission and our mission was half way complete. Jill and I had already finished one of the bottles of Jack and were defiantly feeling the effects from doing so. You have to love Jack, if getting fucked up is your goal Jack will never let you down. Half of the time the damn bottle should come with bail money taped to the side of it. Jill and I pulled up to Ike's

Lake, a private lake outside of Wayne and unlock the gate. As we drove down the lane towards the lake I was feeling excited. Not only was I getting a good drunk tonight, it looked as if I may be getting laid tonight as well. Once out of the car I started a small bonfire in one of the fire pits. I find that little in life is better than a fire under the stars along with strong drink and good company.

Jill and I sat looking up at the stars. Here in North East Nebraska you can see the stars like in few other places, even the Milky Way. Did you know that out in western Nebraska there is a region that is considered to be one of the darkest places on earth, crazy huh? Jill and I lay on a blanket looking up at the Milky Way, passing a joint between us. I loved looking up at the stars. I closed my eyes, the only other place that I have ever seen stars so clearly was in Afghanistan, possibly in Iraq as well but damn were they beautiful in the mountains of Afghanistan.

As to why I know how the stars were so beautiful in the mountains of Afghanistan, I was a sniper in both Iraq and Afghanistan, even in a few places I can't talk about. I remember doing Halo Jumps, just my spotter and I. We would jump deep into the mountains of Afghanistan, Pakistan, Iran, I never really knew exactly where I was going. I knew my targets, I knew my routes, I knew my extraction points, I didn't care about anything else. If you have ever been in the Military you know the drill, go here, go there, here is you target, get to the chopper. That was my job and I was good at my job, really good. The type of confrontation didn't matter to me, hand to hand or taking you out from a mile away. I always took out my targets, I do not believe in failure. One hundred and forty six, that is my confirmed kill's number. Remember this does not count shit I can't talk about. My ex called me a serial killer who got a paycheck once, I like to say I was just good at my job, a good soldier.

Yet how good am I is the question? I mean fuck look where I ended up. Jill and I sat drinking and smoking our joint, oblivious to the world around us. If I would have had a line in the water I would have been in heaven. As we sat drinking the second bottle for a single moment I thought that I heard a sound in the trees. It wasn't but a little over a year ago I was so in touch with nature that I would have noticed any noise out of place. Any smell that wasn't supposed to be there, I was like an animal in the wild, as a good sniper should be. I heard a sound that I knew, the sound of a twig snapping under a man's boot.

I looked up for a second knowing something was wrong. Then I felt what was like a powerful punch in the side of my neck, then another one. As I fell out of consciousness I looked over at Jill, she had a dart in her neck as well. My head began to spin, I felt myself hit the ground with the back of my head, but that was it. The next thing I knew I was waking up in the fucked up love child of the horror movies Saw and Deliverance. So I guess the rest of the story can begin now, or the story as I remember it anyway.

Chapter 3

I opened the door expecting to run straight into the pack of hillbillies on the porch. I peek around the corners looking for anyone at all. I use all of the stealth techniques I had ever learned back in the Army. Secure that I am alone I make my way back into the cabin. I need to pillage any supplies that I can find in order to make my escape. I had already taken the boys knife, I only wish that I could have found a fucking gun. Sadly despite my searching everywhere inside of that little shit hole there were no guns to be found. I laughed to myself, I thought all hillbillies carried a shot gun and a banjo after the age of five? I guess once again the movies had lied. I was able to scrounge up

two more knives and some old water bottle which
I quickly filled with water before making my way
out the door.

All of my training seemed to come back to
me at once. I am working off of pure muscle
memory now. For a few moments I have what I
guess you would call flash back, I can honestly
say that I feel like I am back in the war. I
make my way to a small hill and quickly survey
the land around me. As I look out over the land
I am in awe of its beauty. This is Nebraska by
the way. A sea of green covers the land in all
directions. Fields of corn and beans, the back
bone of the world's diet, all grown here in
Nebraska. Now this is not what I was looking
for, just a bit of an eye opener if you will. As
I look out over the land I am hoping to see a
water tower or a sign of any town that I may

know. I was kidnapped at Ike's Lake. This means that whoever kidnapped Jill and I is most likely from the Region.

Remember how I told you how beautiful it was here just a few moment ago? Well I wasn't lying to you at all, but it does have one huge drawback, it all looks the damn same. Looking out over the land you really have no damn clue as to where the fuck you are. Yes I can tell direction by the sun but that doesn't tell me shit as to where the hell I actually am. I couldn't even see a gravel road at all, only what we call around here a minimum maintenance road. I so wanted to see a real road, some concrete. If I could see a real road I could get the hell out of here, find help, get the damn cops, and go home and have a beer. Who am I kidding I can't call the cops. No, not after

what I just did. I didn't just kill that boy I
mutilated him, I would go down for manslaughter
at least. I only really have one option here,
kill these fuckers and then figure it all out
after. In the Army they taught us, when in
doubt, kill. Yeah, that's the right thing to do,
hell that is what God would want me to do. If I
kill these fucking hillbillies I will save lives
thus that would be doing a good thing, right? I
will be doing the Lords work. I am a warrior, a
warrior for God, yeah that is what I am. I am
not sure which God at this exact moment, I will
decide that later. Four targets that is my
mission that is why God put me here right now.

I take a deep breath and survey the land
once again. I can see an area that drops down
into the earth. Perfect a creek, I can make a
base of operations under the cover of the trees

and the tall weeds. The corn is tall but not tall enough to hide without crouching. I can feel the with drawls from the booze starting to creep over my body. My whole body aches, it's not painful just an annoying ache. I hate the fact that I have with drawls from booze, I am killing myself with the booze, yet I can die without it, fucked up catch twenty two. My weakness is not avoiding pain, my weakness, the reason I drink, is dealing with reality. The booze, well the booze keeps the demons at bay. When I drink I don't think, I don't remember, when I drink the booze I don't want to kill. Without the booze, I am a demon, I remember each kill, I remember how much I enjoyed killing, I know how much I want to kill again. I take a deep breath in and count to five as I inhale, I exhale the same one, two, three, four, and five.

Come into focus, come into focus, I tell myself. What is around you, where are your hides? Where is the best possible location for an ambush?

I am hot, it has to be eighty five degrees outside with a humidity level to match the temperature. The morning mist has all but faded away above the fields. Those bastards will be back soon. Once they see what I have done I know they are going to try and hunt me down, hell I would hunt me down. I had to wait for them, find a good hide, and ambush them one by one. I'm excited these guys hunt people, just like I do. The hunters get to be the hunted, everything is full circle, beautiful. A lion must hunt other lions if only to allow himself to remember that he is a lion. I can't get Jill out of mind. I had lost plenty of buddies in battle, even some by freak accidents, but never like this. I just kept seeing those bastards raping her, that kid killing her, gutting her like a god damn deer. That little freak eating a piece of her still warm liver.

I was thrown back to the war, I am far from innocent. I am guilty of rape, I am very defiantly guilty of murder. I have never eaten human flesh though, that is honestly the only line that I haven't crossed, not that I haven't thought about it though. North of Tikrit we came across a village, just my spotter and I. The moment we walked into the village I could feel every eye upon us. I hated them all, just as they hated me. You see we try and say that we are better than the enemy, but were not. We say that we are there to install freedom, to capture terrorist, insurgents, what the fuck ever. The reality is it is us who defines who is an insurgent or a terrorist. For me anyone who fought for the old regime is an insurgent or anyone who does not accept our presence in their shit hole country is a terrorist. Yet this is not the truth, or the whole truth anyway. The truth is that I am the insurgent, I am the terrorist. We are the invaders here, we are killing innocents every day. If they were in my country and the tables would be turned I would fight them any way I could. In the end we are both wrong, yet we are both right, a no win situation.

My spotter and I made our way into a little shop and purchased a few bottles of water and a couple of bottles of coke. It is crazy I have been all over the world and no matter where I find myself I can always find a bottle of coke, a tiny taste of home. I was watching out the

small door way, all of the shops were closing
their doors. I figured that the meant trouble,
but I didn't care. Fuck with me and I will call
a drone strike in on your little village and
send you even further into the fucking Stone
Age. I had no issue with turning a these savages
mud hut homes into dust.

Little bitch is pretty hot, my spotter said
looking at the serving girl. Yeah she is, I'd
say that she is at least eighteen, I love those
big brown eyes, I laughed. My spotter was right
the girl was pretty hot and had a nice ass
little body on her. I have always been partial
to medium skin tone girls and brown eyes.

Hey sexy girl do you fuck for money, my
spotter asked the girl? I laughed, well if she
does I am paying for some of that ass, I called

out to my spotter. Fuck you American pigs, the young girl scoffed at the two of us with her thick Arabic accent. The girl went right up to my spotter and spit in his face. Fucking cunt, he called out as he jumped to his feet. With one swing of his arm my spotter smacked the girl so hard she fell straight to the dirt floor within the store. Hey bro close that door and keep watch, my spotter told me. I am about to have some fun with this fucking whore, he laughed.

You won't fuck for money huh whore, he yelled as he ripped the girl's clothes off. I bet you will fuck for free, he laughed. Damn bro look at this little fucking Sand Nigger bitches body man, sexy as fuck, he called out. I looked down on the naked girl on the floor attempting to fight off my spotter, he was right she had one hell of a body. The girl tried to call out but my spotter then punched her in the face breaking her jaw. With these war time formalities all taken care of my spotter began to rape the young girl. God damn this pussy is tight, he called out, you need to get yourself some of this brother, he laughed.

I should have looked down upon what was going on in front of me in horror and disgust, but I didn't. War does things to a man, bad things. After a while things that you never thought you would do, hell, never be able to do just become the norm. I should have told my spotter to get off of the girl. The truth was I was excited and couldn't wait to feel how good this girl's pussy was going to feel when I took my turn raping her. I sat there and watched my spotter pound this poor girl for the next ten minutes. I was impressed he lasted so long, I couldn't remember the last time that I had the pleasure of enjoying some pussy. It had to have been at least a year. The last time was at a whore house in Germany, some hot girl from Norway, yeah that was it. My only hope was that I lasted longer than two minuet's with this girl before I busted my nut.

I got on top of the girl as soon as my spotter had finished. I won't lie to you, it felt good to push myself inside of her. She was young and her pussy was still really tight, far tighter than that hookers had been. As I raped her I looked down on her, she was crying. I was sure that she was in agony, I just didn't care.

I told myself it was every woman's fantasy to be raped. Repeating this to myself I enjoyed looking down on her as I raped her. It took me almost ten minuet's to bust my nut, good hang

time after a year of no pussy I thought. It felt

good to cum, real good. Fuck this stupid little

bitch, fucking rag head, I thought. This bitch

was nothing more than a spoil of war in my eyes.

These fucking rag heads weren't even people in

my eyes anymore. How many friends had I already

lost to these fucks, probably this bitches

family members?

I pulled my pants up and buttoned them

along with fixing my belt. Look at that piece of

shit whore, my spotter said looking down on the

naked girl rolled into a ball on the dirt floor.

Fuck that whore, I said. I grabbed her by her

hair and took out my knife. I slashed her throat

with my blade, tell Allah I sent you whore, I

laughed as I let her body fall to the dirt

floor. If you were a virgin before today tell

him it was my honor to ensure that you were no prize for some piece of shit terrorist, I laughed. My spotter pulled out his dick and pissed all over the body, one last insult.

I would love to be able to tell you that was the last time that my spotter and I ever raped and killed a woman, but I can't. Forty six, Forty six is the number of women that we raped and killed during our time in Iraq and Afghanistan. After a while it just became the norm really, something fun to do. We were known as the most vicious two man crew out there. Personally I felt it was a lot of exaggeration, but I liked fame none the same. We did have hundreds of kills under our belts, only half of which confirmed at best. We were good at our jobs even if our methods were a bit unorthodox. The brass all looked the other way as long as they saw results they didn't care what the fuck we did. My spotter and I took heads, we impaled bodies hell we even crucified people now and again. We raped and killed females as often as we could. Men, women, children, none were safe, everyone is a target, there are no innocents in war just targets all looking to kill you first.

After a while you lose touch with any sort of former reality. War, well before you realize it you just become war. War and all its horrors become a part of who you are, hell becomes who you are. Killing, killing is so damn easy, it really takes no effort at all.

You know what the hard part was for me, it wasn't killing people, it wasn't being out in some damn wasteland, it wasn't death, it wasn't the damn war itself, no it was coming home. Once you get home a whole new world of things are expected of you. The world expects that you will be normal in their eyes, an average Joe. The world expects that you will get a job, be a citizen, start a family, buy a house, have some rug rats you know, normal people shit. You have to block out who you now are, the monster that you have become, be the old you, a new you, a better you. It is hard, you can't forget, no one who wasn't there understands that you just can't forget. I did a lot of fucked up shit over there. I am guilty of sins against man and God. I am guilty of shit that would impress Vlad fucking Dracula himself. Do I stay up at night thinking about it all? Well, let's just say that is why I drink.

Chapter 4

Now outside I made my way down to the creek as fast as I possibly could. I looked around, I needed a hide. I saw a large tree covered in thick canopy of leaves. I quickly made my way up the tree and scanned the terrain. The tree allowed me to have a visual over the entire area including the cabin. These fucks will be back soon, real soon. As soon as the see the work that I made of their little brother they will be after me. This is exactly what I am hoping for, let them hunt me, let the sheep come to the wolf.

I took off my red shirt and buried it in the mud. I began to cover my entire body with mud. I did this first to help camouflage myself,

and secondly to keep any bugs from biting me.
Camo is always the key, you must become one with
whatever environment that you find yourself in.
Rule one, if you are not one hundred percent a
part of your environment you will be discovered,
no exceptions. It only takes a split second to
go from predator to prey. I was taught to always
look at the animals in the environment that I
found myself in. All one need do is to look at
the animals, they will always show you the
camouflage that you need to survive. You don't
need much, just enough to break up your shape
really.

I was surprised at how well I was able to
climb the tree. It had been a long time since I
had to climb a tree to get my bearings. The last
time had been in the mountains of Afghanistan. I
stayed in that damn tree as still as a branch

for two damn days before I got my shot, but I got my shot. You only need to know two things to be a sniper. First how to shoot the course if you will, you must be able to hit your target. Next and this is the hardest of all, you must have patience. You have to be like a Buddhist Monk, meditating for days, never moving. That is the key the ability to wait, wait in silence, never moving, never losing sight of the end goal. The ability to sit and focus on your target then take your target and still not move until you have to, well in my eyes it's an art. The killing part that is easy for a sniper, anyone really. I always felt it wasn't much different than hunting deer. I always enjoyed it honestly, the whole thing is fun to me. The hunt, the stalking, sitting in silence, then finally taking down your target, it's a rush I just can't explain.

These guys were going to pay, Jill was my friend, my confident, even my lover. Jill was the closest person I had in life who cared about me just for me. Jill never judged me, she never wanted me to tell her about my past, she just understood me. Now Jill is gone, raped and murdered by a pack of hillbillies. I could still hear and see her entrails splash into the bucket when the boy field dressed her. I could hear her blood trickling down from her body into the bucket. I could still see all of them taking turns on her, all of them raping her. Jill's muffled cries for help haunted me.

In my tree watching the cabin in silence I thought about the boy that I had killed. How his body tensed up as I cut his cock and balls from his body. The feel of his warm blood as it covered my hands, the smell of death in the air. That look in his eyes as I shoved his cock and balls down his throat. He knew it was all over then, he saw, he felt death coming for him as he choked on what would have someday been his manhood. I thought about how easy it was to cut through his spinal cord. It's always easier to behead the young, the spinal cord just cuts easier. When I took his head his blood would have sprayed like a fountain had I not castrated him first. Thinking of all this gave my body a giant warm fuzzy. You know what I am talking about, like that feeling you get when you kiss a girl for the first time or vice a versa. That is the feeling that I have, the feeling of joy and excitement all at once.

I sat in the tree in silence watching the cabin. My cover was so good I knew that I would never be detected. I began making myself a spear from a limb that I had cut. I decided that I would kill each one of these fucks, one by one. Unless I could get a gun I would do it with blades and my spear, let them suffer. A gun would be too merciful in all truth, mercy is for God, not me. I have no clue if killing these guys would be Gods work, or the work of the Devil, I don't care. All I know is that I will show no mercy, I doubt they had for any of their victims. I looked out over the land, maybe I am an Angel, I thought? What is an Angel but a Demon by another name? Heaven won the war right? So as I see it Heaven wrote the history, thus those Angels on the losing side became Demons. We all know that the history is written by the

winners. It is the same as any war in my eyes,
one man's terrorist is another man's freedom
fighter. So maybe I am a demon sent by Satan to
do the Devils work, I get confused in my own
head. Yes that may just be it I am here to do
the Devils work, clean up one of God's messes.
As I see it the Devil just got a bad rap anyway.
You see the Devil was never evil. In fact it was
or is his job to punish evil. Yet if I am made
in God's image, as is the Devil he nor I can be
evil, right?

I have tried to be a different man, a
better man. I tried not to kill people, to rape
women, to murder, I really did it just never
worked for me. One day I just realized that it
was all a part of who I am, good or bad. The day
I realized this I just went with it, went all
out. I quit trying to hide who I was and in a

war zone, well men like me are needed. I am the man that God intended me to be, made in his image. Thus I am not evil, I am not even good, I just am, like God, I am indifferent. I am in essence God's delivery man. It is my job to deliver souls to be judged as fast as pizzas are delivered to one's home.

I sat in silence, only the sounds of the birds filled the air. I remember when I lived in Las Vegas for a while, you never heard the birds, no nature really, just city noise. I sat in my tree listening, I heard a noise that was out of place, the sound of a truck off in the distance. I could tell it was on the minimum maintenance road due to the lack of the sounds of gravel beneath the tires. The small dust cloud halted at the top of the lane as the truck turned down and drove towards the cabin. I quickly made my way down from my tree and into the cornfield towards the cabin. Without thinking I used the old crouch method they taught us back in boot camp.

This movement allows you the greatest amount of speed while using a zigzag pattern. You run crouched over then lay on your belly, take a lay of the land then repeat. This method works, works good. I only saw one man get out of the truck, one of the brothers. Well that is what I suspected they were. The man took no notice of me at all, I studied him like scripture. He was around six foot tall, medium build, dark hair, blue eyes, bad teeth, bad skin, smelled of booze and cigarettes, and was blaring some really bad country music. I mean bad, not the good Hank Williams or Johnny Cash, no this was the Keith Urban type crap. I laughed to myself, idiot could have at least been playing some Garth Brooks.

I lay not five feet from the fool, hidden by the mud, the corn, and the shadows. The smart move would be to kill him the moment he stepped out of the truck. I should kill him quick before he has the chance to fight back. This would be the smart move, but I want him to suffer first, know he is dying. This man is one of the fucks that raped and murdered Jill, my only true friend that I had left. I already told you mercy is for God. My plan was to make each one of these deaths epic, some real horror movie type shit.

I studied my prey as he exited his old Ford truck. I could smell him distinctly now, I would say he hadn't showered in days. He wreaked of sweat, not just any sweat but sweat mixed with booze and a bad diet. You would be surprised how one's diet dictates their body odor. I could smell the Arab spices in a man's sweat a mile away back in Iraq and Afghanistan. I was usually alone in the bush back in Afghanistan especially, I took pride in knowing all of the smells in nature. In Afghanistan and Iraq one need only hold his nose to the air to detect the scent of mint or curry to know the enemy was close. The slightest whiff and you knew that you were not alone. I am sure they sniffed the air for the smells of American spices. Often I chose

only to eat what I found in nature when there,

to smell of my surroundings as much as possible.

You know what always gave the enemy away to me

via their odor, the smell of their teas that

they drank, they all drank a lot of tea thus

they smelled of it.

As I stated before my foe was around six

foot tall, medium build, yet not fat at all. You

could tell just by looking at him and the slight

hunch in his posture that he had worked hard all

of his life. A man that has worked hard all of

his life has a certain look to him, a bit more

rugged if you will. I could smell the booze on

him, cheap vodka mixed with beer. I could also

smell the chemical smell on him that only came

from smoking meth. Fucking tweakers, I never got

that shit at all. You see I like to both sleep

and eat, meth is not conducive to either one of these activities. For real though, why the fuck would you want to get all twacked out in small town Nebraska. There isn't shit to do here! Why the hell would you want to be all twacked out, no possibility of sleeping and fucking nothing to do? The mere thought of this escapes all logic to me. In reality that is the type of shit we would do back in the war to torture you. As I see it you can only watch so much damn TV in a day. The movie channels recycle the same shit every few hours that is torture in my eyes. Oh well I guess that is just not meant for me or for me to understand. I am not meant to understand some things at all, I accept this fact.

Covered in mud I blended in perfectly with the dark Nebraska soil of the cornfield. I looked of the earth, I smelled of the earth, I am of the earth. The idea of this hunt and now the reality of this hunt had me excited. It had been far too long since I was able to put my unique talents to use. My plan was to let the bastard go into the house, I wanted him to see what was left of his little brother.

My target called out.

"Skippy, Skippy where the fuck are you boy?"

The lack of a return answer had left the poor fool with a puzzled look on his face. As he walked up the stairs into the cabin his large boots made a loud clomping sound.

"Skippy, what the hell you doing in there boy, you best not be fucking that girl. You best a have that bitch dressed and ready."

He called out as he got to the door. I couldn't wait for him to open the door, the anticipation was almost too damn much for me.

As my foe walked in the door I made my move. In a matter of seconds I was on the porch, doing so in utter silence.

"Skippy!"

My prey screamed out at the top of his lungs.

"What the fuck, what the fuck?"

He called out over and over again. I caught a glimpse of my prey on his knee's holding the head of his little brother in his hands. I silently picked up a steel crowbar that was on the porch. My prey was crying like a little bitch holding his dead little brother's head in

his hands as if it were part of a broken doll.
In silence, I used the shadows, I am invisible I
do not exist. I am right behind my prey, with a
quick swing of the crowbar I smash it against my
foes temple. In an instant the fool drops like a
load of bricks to the floor.

I quickly take the rope that had previously
been used on Jill and tie up my victim. I went
into his pocket and pulled his cell phone from
his pocket. His brothers would be calling soon I
was sure, I was excited to answer the phone for
him. I quickly took some photos of the dead
little brother as well as the brother that I had
tied up.

Wasting no time I drug my tied up foe
outside. I tied him up just how we did prisoners
back in the war. It's a combination of a loop

with knots almost making a handle if you will at
the feet. This makes it really easy to drag your
prisoner where you need them with little to no
resistance. Even with this idiots size he was
easy to drag through the cornfield. I purposely
left a trail even an idiot could follow for the
remaining brothers to follow me into the
cornfield. My prisoner was still out cold as I
drug him towards the creek. I was having fun,
yet I almost longed for a small little fight at
least. I was sure that would come later whether
I wanted it or not. I remembered them saying
that they would be back to cook later. Three
more hours or so at best, I thought.

I got to the edge of the creek, it was
twenty feet or so to the bottom. All of the
trees were on the top of the creek wall which is
where I wanted to be. I looked over all of the

trees looking for the perfect one to utilize my plan. It didn't take long for me to decide on a small cotton wood maybe only five years old. I quickly took my prisoner and tied him up to the tree tying his arms out crucifixion style. I then tied his legs to the tree making sure that he was one hundred percent secure. I had done this same thing to at least one hundred prisoners back in the war so that we could interrogate them, so I guess you can say that I am a professional at this type of thing. I always got all of the Intel that I needed. Torture, they say that it is illegal, a bunch of hippie, liberal, just pussy Geneva Convention bullshit. To this I say tell the enemy this. The enemy could care less about some bullshit Geneva Convention, for them torture is the norm. To be honest many of the tactics I used in the war I learned from them. The truth is I am good at torturing people, I actually enjoy it.

For me torture is simple, I just separate myself from what I was doing. Well, at first anyway, after a while I just began to enjoy doing it. I would pretend I was Dean from Super Natural. I would pretend I was him when he became hell's main torturer. Dean enjoyed his work, no matter how brutal he had to be, as do I. Torture is needed, it is a simple tool in my tool chest, and I use it well. You see the enemy knows that you have a set of rules to follow that in the end you won't really do shit to them. More so they knew that if they ended up in one of our prisons they would actually be living far better than they ever had before. An enemy that has no fear of you will never give up any information. The enemy must not only think that you will do something, they must know that you will. If I am holding your wife in front of you and I say that I will slit her throat and then not do it after a while the enemy knows that I am bluffing. Yet if after a while of you holding out I cut her throat so deep that I nearly take her head off the enemy begins to understand the seriousness of his situation. Thus after I kill your wife and now hold his children in front of him, he knows I will cut their throats as well. This is what motivates a prisoner to talk. The funny thing is that in the end I will kill you and your whole family anyway, kids and all. Remember when you take out a nest of rodents or pest you do not differentiate between adults and children, you just take out the nest.

My prisoner, my victim secured to the tree closest to the water's edge I begin my work. I quickly cut off all of the prisoners clothes. I cut a piece of the shirt and stuffed it into his mouth to muffle his screams. I was sick of waiting for this fool to wake up so I splashed his face with water till he woke up. As he came to he was slowly shaking his head trying to figure out just what had happened and what was going on. It wasn't that long ago that I was in pretty much the same situation, thus I knew his feelings well. My new friend came to and looked at me scared and confused. I love the look a fear in a man's eyes. When a man is truly terrified his pupils will grow three to four times their normal size. Even with this poor fools eyes being blue they damn near looked black with the size of his pupils.

I grabbed my prisoner by the face.

"Well hello there my friend."

I laughed looking into his eyes.

"So right now you are probably wondering just how the hell all of this has transpired?"

I laughed as I snapped a photo of him with his phone.

"Well buddy this time you picked the wrong damn one. Now I do not have any clue as to how many people you and the rest of your retarded family have killed over the years but I do assure you that Jill was the last one. That was her name, Jill, she was the one that you all raped then had that little inbreed gut like a fucking deer."

I told him gripping his face.

The prisoner is trying to talk to me.

"Oh you have something to say do you. Fuck it, why not I will let you have your say, just know that if you try and scream I will cut your tongue out of your mouth and throw it to the catfish in the creek."

I laughed.

"I am sure you remember what I did with your little inbred brother, don't forget those cock and balls in his mouth."

I laughed as I pulled his gag out.

"You mother fucker you killed my brother. He was just a boy goddamn it, just a fucking boy!"

He cried out.

"Yes, yes I did kill your brother, I enjoyed killing him to, you see he was just a boy, yet he was a boy that would grow into who and what you are, thus he had to die. That so called boy raped and field dressed my friend and was eating a chunk of her liver when I killed him. It was fun killing your baby brother, he didn't put up much of a fight, little pussy really."

I laughed in my prisoners face.

"You know he cried like a little girl, begging me not to kill him, that is when I cut his baby sized cock and balls off and shoved them down his bitch ass throat. He died chocking on his own cock and balls. It took a while to since he had such a small ass dick."

I laughed again, egging on my prisoner.

"He was still alive when I took his head from his body you know that right? You know they say that the brain lives for eight top twelve minuet's after death. That is why I left his eyes open, I wanted him to see everything. I guess he got to see everything as I hung his head from the ceiling for you to find, did you like that one?"

"Fuck you, you, sick son of a bitch!"

"Me sick, are you fucking kidding me, you are the fucking rapist cannibals man, I don't fucking eat people. Now that shit is sick, I just kill people man."

"My brothers are going to kill your fucking ass mother fucker, they will hunt you down like a dog and kill you."

"Are you actually crying you little bitch? Pathetic, you know that I am going to kill you, and you know that I will not be doing it in a

nice and painless way. I suggest that you spend
your last moments in life as a man, and take
your death like a man. It is a true honor and
gives reverence to the gods when you accept your
death. Few us of ever take much responsibility
for our lives, but we can with our death."

"Go to hell mother fucker!"

My prisoner cried out.

"Hell, well I believe that hell is right
here on earth, and I am afraid that you my
friend are in it."

I laughed out loud.

"Well brother, damn I can't believe that I
just called you that. How about this, Baby Cakes
our conversation time is now over. It is time

for you to know hell, to know pain, to know terror."

I told my prisoner/victim.

"You see my goal is to show you something deeper than pain. Physical pain is so limiting, just one splash of paint on the canvas really. Back in Afghanistan I made sure my prisoners knew fear before they died, knew that there were things out there worse than death. I have decided that I want you to understand the fear that lays within your own mind, the feeling of being trapped in your own body. I want you to know that you are dying, and know that there is nothing that you can do about it. You see Baby Cakes the pain that exist in the body is nothing compared to hearing your own screams within your very mind."

I laughed once again as I shoved the shirt back into my prisoner's mouth.

"Oh buddy it is time for you to know that hell that you were talking about. You are a hunter, I am sure that there are few in this world that know the game in this little corner of heaven that you do. I myself saw some coyote scat, some badger, a few coon tracks, but that was it, Pretty scary man those badgers are nothing to fuck with."

I laughed.

"Well then Baby Cakes it's off to hell you go."

I told my prisoner.

"You see this blade Baby Cakes, this is the one that I used to butcher and kill your little brother. I used this very blade to cut his cock and balls off. Then it was this blade that I used to kill him and then cut off his head."

With a huge smile I then took my blade and ran it across my prisoner's belly. I pushed with just enough force to cut through the flesh and through the membrane holding his guts inside of his organ cavity.

As his guts fell from his body I laughed. You see these guts Baby Cakes, these are your guts I laughed. My prisoner was freaking out, trying to throw himself from side to side but to no avail, I had him tied to secure. I scooped up some of his intestines in my hand and held them up for him to see. They felt warm and kind of gooey in my hands.

"You like what you are seeing, screaming on the inside aren't you?"

I stretched out his guts letting them rest in the dirt as well as the water. I then made two slits in his bowels allowing for the stench to fill the air.

"Damn that shit smells fucking disgusting, what the hell have you been eating? Now Baby Cakes I have to tell you, you are going to die from this, but you will die slowly, I can't imagine the pain you are in right now? That foul stink filling the air coming from your body that smell is going to attract every predator and scavenger in the area. You eat people, now you will be eaten, seems fitting to me. Damn with this stink I would say every animal in a one hundred square mile has already caught a whiff of your stink. Soon they will all be dining on your guts, while you are alive to feel it, fucked up huh?"

I couldn't help but to burst into laughter.

"Look up there Baby Cakes, do you see those two hawks? They see you, they smell you and to them you are a damn fine lunch. I am going to leave you for a bit, enjoy your death Baby Cakes."

I said this as I made my leave. I patted my prisoner on the back.

"Baby Cakes, I don't know how big of a participant that you were in your actual life, but I assure you that you will be one in your death."

With that said I made my way back into the grove. I quickly scaled my tree getting back into my comfortable hide. I was once again in my perfect lookout point, watching for the brothers as well as watching the show that is Baby Cakes death. I didn't give him two or three hours top before he went septic and died. That was enough time to feel each and every horrific moment of the life he had left.

"Chapter 6"

I sat perched in my tree looking out over the fields awaiting the brother's return. Nature is a beautiful beast, she truly is. You see nature makes everything equal if you will, maybe a better way to put it would be that nature allows nothing to go to waste. Already in what has been just a short hour maybe an hour and a half the mess I had left was already being cleaned up. The entrails of the hillbilly that I had allowed to find their way to the floor of the cold earth were already being devoured by nature. Best for me was watching and knowing that the fucker was still alive, although barely. I wanted to hear his screams yet I wanted him to hear them more, thus I gagged him. No screams are ever louder than the ones inside of one's own head.

Those two hawks that I had seen earlier were already beginning to pick the body clean. I watched with joy as they picked at and tore at my prisoner's entrails. Their powerful beaks and talons were tearing chunk after chunk of flesh free from the body of the still living man. The craw fish had climbed up from the creek bed and began to get their fill as well. His moans and random movement did little to stall nature's cleanup crew. I was really amazed to see a raccoon out in the daylight taking his turn on the entrails as well. Soon the badgers, the coyotes, and all the rest of nature's cleanup crew would come to devour their fill as well. I know what you are thinking right, how fucked up am I? Well to that I say not at all. I am truly amazed at how fast and efficient nature works, it truly is beautiful. Ask yourself how often other than on Discovery Channel does one get to watch nature in all of its glory?

I decided to get down from my perch and leave my nature special to the animals. I knew that there had to be some more weapons in the idiot's truck. In my haste I didn't even take the time to look. It's hot as hell out and the fucking bugs are eating through my now dried and cracked mud exterior. I made my way down the tree and back down to the creek bank to cover myself with fresh mud. As I descend all of the animals begin to scatter, thinking that I to was there for my fill of the feast I am sure. Here I am the top predator, I like how nature respects a pecking order, if only humans understood this concept.

I looked at my dying new friend, I was surprised he had lasted as long as he had. I was even more surprised that none of the animals had made their way to his heart yet.

"How are you doing my friend?"

I felt his weak pulse by holding his actual heart in my hand.

"You know that I could end all of this right now for you."

I laughed as I gripped the heart his little tighter.

"Would you like that man, would you like to give up and just die?"

I grabbed his shirt and soaked it with water and held it to his lips.

"You know the Romans did this for Jesus? Now they didn't do this because they wanted to kill him no, they did this to keep him alive a little bit longer. You see the Romans knew that there was no joy in a man not suffering."

I said this as I gave my prisoner another drink.

"So this being said friend I am going to let you live, not that I think that you will make it much longer. Damn man that fucking craw dad is eating your stomach."

I laughed aloud once again.

"Does this hurt man, or is it more of a mental thing? I hope this hurts you, more so I hope that this hurts your mind. My goal is that you are a part of your own death, that you know it that you feel it coming. My goal is that in your last moments of life you will understand just why it is that I condemned you to death. In an odd way I even want you to take pleasure in your death. Well bro I am off to see what toys you have in your truck, hang in there a bit longer and don't forget all that I have just told you."

I laughed as I walked away. After hopping in the creek and covering my entire body with mud I made my way back up the creek bank and into the corn field. The shade felt good, it was nice and cool between the rows of corn. I could feel all of the sharp leaves of the corn plants brush across my body. Had I not covered myself in mud the leaves of the corn could have really would cut me quite easily. I loved the way it felt to make my way through the corn field. I grew up hiding in cornfields as a kid, playing Army in them. God those were the days, just a bunch of care free kids playing kill the Russians.

I remember one day when Travis and I made our way out into the cornfield to play Army one day. We couldn't have been over ten years old really, hell maybe even younger. We grew up in the eighties, free range parenting was the norm, even more so in our cases. The corn field was ready for harvest, all of the corn stalks being dry and brown. As always we set our so called camp deep in the field, or as deep as we were willing to enter anyway. As always we made our makeshift tepee for shelter. Then thinking that we were super soldiers out on some long mission we made our camp fire. Now this fire had a purpose, we had planned to cook our M.R.E.'s that we had gotten from Travis's dad. Now as you can see all of this was totally innocent young boy shit. The issue came when the reality that we were kids and unable to control our camp fire, especially since everything around us was essentially dry tinder. Of course in just a few moments our fire quickly got out of control. Travis and I tried to put the fire out but to no

avail. Thus, Travis and I did what all young
boys would do, we ran our asses off and got the
hell out of there. I will never forget us
running into a bunch of other kids and joining
in their games as fast as we could to attempt to
attain some sort of alibi. We acted as if we
were surprised when we said, hey look smoke. At
least half of that field burned down that day.
Thankfully Travis and I were never caught and
punished for what we had done. Looking back I am
sure that the farmer got more money from the
insurance claim than he would have selling the
crop. Had the farmer known it was us in all
reality he probably should have thanked us, well
that is if he would have ever known who we were.

Crazy the shit that goes through your head
as you are laying on the ground not knowing how
many more people you will soon be killing. I saw

a large grasshopper next to me, nature's potato chip.

I quickly grabbed him and bit off the tail. The grasshopper was crunchy as I bit down into it, I try not to think about textures when I eat gross shit. Now and again one must get past their preconceived notions of gross and just eat for fuel. I won't lie when you cook them the things are pretty damn good. Raw, well raw is gross but fuck it I need the protein.

I am still fighting the uneasiness of not having any booze in my system. I can't believe that I allowed myself to sink so damn low these past few years. I had allowed myself to become a drunk just like my father was before me. Yet in a fucked up way it brought me closer to him. I believe in our shared addiction that in a way I understood him, understood why he did what he did, if that makes any sense at all. As I hold my stomach I pledge that I will not drink again, at least never to excess again. I feel as though I have given up all self-respect. I have lost everything in my drunkenness. In my drunkenness I have lost who I am, who God intended me to be.

I looked out over the road, it's clear. I ran up to my still suffering prisoner's truck. The first thing that I noticed made me almost want to vomit. I know I have seen and done some gross shit but this sick fuck had a soda bottle filled with tobacco spit. That shit always grosses me out more than anything on this earth. I have never gotten this shit at all. How is it, that anyone in this day and age could ever pick up such a filthy habit, I just don't understand. Looking past the disgusting bottle I rummaged through the truck looking for weapons. I opened

the glove box and bingo, a loaded forty five, a

very nice 1911 to be precise, my favorite model

of forty five of all time. I have always loved

the 1911, the 1911 is like a shark, perfect from

its inception. I kept digging and found a nice

hunting knife in the piles of trash that filled

the truck. Lastly I found a bag of unopened

nacho cheese Doritos. Not that these would do

much for me health wise but I am hungry as shit

and this bag of Doritos is calories.

I made my way back into the house for one

last look around. I had left in a haste, there

is a possibility I left something behind in my

in my rush. My water bottles were getting low, I

needed to replenish them. The lack of booze and

water had me pretty dehydrated. I opened the

door, the stench of the boy's body hit me like a

brick in the face. Death has a smell, a horrible smell that only one who knows death can truly describe. I look at the boy's body, the head now on the floor. I wish that someone could have allowed that boy to have lived a normal life. Sadly he was born into one fucked up nest of animals. I picked up the boys head.

"Sorry kid, I had no choice but to kill you but don't fret, soon all of your brothers will be with you to keep you company."

I started looking for any weapons once again, possibly some more ammo even. I had my spear that I had made, a few knives, and now my 1911, but I really wanted a rifle. Sadly as I searched one more time I didn't find any rifles at all. I did find a bow and some arrows, not a great bow but it would do the job. My plan was to wound them, then pick them off one by one. I wanted to be able to torture them all, let them know they were dying, make them pay for what they had done. I drank two bottles of water before refilling them. As I left the cabin I noticed three cans of diesel fuel, I couldn't use them now but took a mental note for later.

I made an obvious trail from the road into the field that even an idiot could follow, let alone these bastards. I wanted these son of a bitches to find their brother, only I hoped that the coyotes got to him first. These bastards ate people, I wanted them to see what it looked like when one of their own flesh and blood had been eaten. Psychological warfare can be far more effective than a bullet. My goal was to see how strong these boy's minds were, let alone their hearts. I made my way back to my hide, this time along the high ground, to make multiple trails.

I have my camo on now, I am one with nature, one

with the Nebraska landscape. I am a hunter and

now like a hunter I am simply playing the

waiting game, patience is the greatest of

virtues.

"Chapter 7"

I close my eyes for just a mere second, I

am not quite sure but I may have actually fallen

asleep. I am in a house, but the house is not my

house at all. No this place looked like one of

those houses on that whatever alley street on

Harry Potter. I try to get out of the house but

the door is locked, so I climb out of the

window. When I looked up there is a three headed

horse with Zena the Warrior Princess riding it. Zena is throwing fireballs at me and doing that awful yodel thing she does on the show the entire time.

I make my way across the roof hoping to jump to the ground. I look over to my side and see an owl. The owl looks just like The Great Owl from that Secret of Nimh Cartoon from when I was a kid. I am memorized by the owl I can't take my eyes off of him. Right before I jump the owl looks at me with his huge golden eyes.

"Hey buddy I don't think that I wouldn't do that if I were you."

The owl says to me. I look at the owl and ask.

"Why not?"

"If you go that way it will lead you straight to hell. Now and again we have to muster up all of our courage and stand our ground and fight. Win or lose doesn't matter as long as you fight with heart. In the end all that matters is that you had the balls to fight in the first place."

"Your right owl, you are right."

I wake up knowing what the owl had meant, as well as knowing that I watch way too many movies while intoxicated. Since I had gotten home from the military I had tried to run from all that I had seen, all that I had done while at war. I have been afraid of the man that I had become, possibly I was even ashamed. I have been using drugs and booze to hide from who I am, who I am supposed to be. I thought that I hated myself, yet I knew nothing was further from the truth. No I have been trying to live up to what everyone else wanted, what everyone else expected me to be. The truth is that I am not the same man that I was when I left my small Nebraska town. It took the world to make me grow, to turn me into a man. It took the world to turn me into the man that I am supposed to be. The reality is that no matter how much I try I will never be able to run away from the man that I am. I will never be able to run away from my truth. No matter what drugs I take, no matter how much booze I drink, eventually I will sober up. Once sober I will have to face reality. It is now or never, follow the words of the owl, no point in putting off what is certain. I will follow the owl, as fucked up as that sounds.

Despite the great words from the owl I left once again asking myself, am I crazy?

I open my eyes, I am laying in the dirt. I can feel the cold earth beneath me, the cool shade from the cornstalks protecting me from the sun. Laying on the earth covered in mud I couldn't be much closer to the earth than I am now. I look out on the road hoping to see my prey. The sun is setting lower in the sky, the darkness of the night will soon protect me. I am night, I am darkness, I the demon in the night. Soon, soon I will be the man that God intended me to be. Soon I will be doing God's work.

I listen to the sounds of nature all around me. One must come to an almost meditative state when in the wilderness. Once you reach this state only then can you begin to become on with nature. Once you reach this point any noise out of place will be noticed. We all have this ability within us, only we have chosen to forget it. Most of us just choose to ignore our primitive survival instincts. I assure you that one day you will need them, so my advice is hone them now before it's too late. Too many people are afraid of the natural world, to use to their comfort and luxury. People have all become so urban that when they see anything not made of concrete or red brick their bodies fill with fear. What is truly more scary, the fear of a random predator, or getting mugged by a different type of predator? You have forgotten that you are the top predator, the top of the food chain. A mugger, a coyote, hell a fucking twacked out hillbilly, all equally prey.

There is a cloud of dust in the air over the top of the road. A smile begins to cover my face thinking of the fun that is soon to come. Soon I will be killing these fools one by one, each and every one of them. I take a deep breath in, am I the Angel of Death I ask myself? Am I doing God's work or is this just revenge, I ask myself? If I am not doing God's work then whose work am I doing?

Is there a God at all? The same damn question I have always asked myself. I have had far too much time to contemplate this damn question, the abstract concept that is God. Hunkered down in the mud, one with the cold earth often for days at a time, well this is the type of shit you ask yourself. When waiting for days to kill a man, take out a target whatever, you ask yourself if you may just be doing some shit God may not approve of. When all you have to do is think, well let's keep it real shit can get scary. I have often thought of myself as the Buddha when he sat under the Bodhi tree. I cannot count the amount of times I have lost myself in deep meditation. I am enlightened, I am the Buddha, I am the hand of God, I am one with the entire universe.

People ask why do bad things happen to good people? Well first and foremost there are no truly good people. No one out there is innocent, not even you. No the truth is that the Gods, God what the hell ever want you call him has no clue what it is to truly be alive. You must know joy, love, and happiness to understand this. Yet, what are these things without pain, heart break, and sadness, pain has helped me to remember that I am alive far to many times? The reality of life is confusion at best. The trick is getting past this confusion, seeing things clearly for the first time if you will. This is why I meditate, to get past all of the confusion, to see through my own shit covered binoculars I know to be my own ego. Meditation allows me to see something deeper than most. I have ascended, I am no longer even a human being really, not as you perceive one anyway. I now look at everyone else knowing that you are all below me, but still my equal in every way. Yet I know that I am no longer a part of the same species group as you. I have evolved past the idea of looking for god, I am now a God myself.

The truck is loud, an old F250 four door. The piece of shit truck has a bad exhaust, the fumes cut through the smells of the natural world like a knife. It is almost sickening really, all of those toxic fumes polluting this pristine air here in my Nebraska countryside. The truck is a rusty with hints of old blue paint peeking through here and there. I don't know why but I hate this truck, it kind of reminds me of the type of shit you would see back in Afghanistan or Iraq, maybe that is it? I don't know just how they got the trucks over there, it seemed they had all of our left overs. It made me smile remembering just how many rounds I had put into the windshields of trucks that looked just like this one.

Four guys got out of the truck. Only one of them is a big fella, but I know that size of a man is not a measure of the size of the fight a man has with him. The big fella is maybe six foot three, and two hundred plus pounds. He is missing his two front teeth, typical. I never understood why these hicks were so damn afraid to go the dentist. The big fella has dirty brown hair peeking out of his Huskers hat. I will have to kill him first. This is one of my rules, take out the biggest man first. He poses the greatest risk, often even if he isn't the best fighter others look up to him due to his size. Take out this target first, the big man always holds more danger than just their size. I will make him suffer none the less.

The second guy is a bit smaller, maybe five foot eight. I wouldn't give him more than a buck fifty weight wise. His hair is blonde and in a long pony tail going down his back. This dip shit is wearing a wife beater, so damn white trash it hurts to look at. I have to admit, I like his shoes, a nice pair of Nike Air Max. I will have to check the size after I kill him. I know it is hopeful at best though, I wear a size

thirteen. I made a mental note, try not to get

blood on those shoes.

The third dude is around five foot ten. He

is bigger than the other I would give him maybe

one hundred seventy five pounds, a pretty decent

size dude overall. He looks like he is going to

be fun to kill, I may even get a good fight out

of him. His hair is dark, he has a really long

and scraggly beard. In a way he reminded me of

the hillbilly from that show Moonshiners that

worked with that Josh dude till they had a

fight. I wonder if any of these guys makes

moonshine? I always wanted to make moonshine. I

could be like old Popcorn Sutton, living in the

hills playing my guitar and my banjo. I have

always felt that lifestyle would just really

suit me. After I kill everyone maybe I will look

around and see if these guys have a still anyplace around.

The last of the four guys is the smallest of them all, maybe five foot six tops. If this little dude weighed over a buck and a quarter I would be surprised. Yet like I said a man's size does not measure the fight within him, never take a man's size for granted. These little fuckers usually all have the Napoleon complex, little guys always feel they have something to prove. Did you know that Napoleon really wasn't that short at all? In fact he was actually quite average in size in comparison to his own men. Just like I always thought that Vikings were damn near giants. The reality was that most were maybe five foot eight to ten tops. Yet I guess if I were five foot one and I had to fight a man near six foot tall he would be a giant in my eyes. Fuck it to the point his size does not matter, he is already dead, they are all already dead. Soon they will only know it is all.

I watch the four men from my hide in the dirt. Covered in mud laying on the dark earth I am invisible. Soon these four mother fuckers will be worm food, food for all of the animals of North East Nebraska. If all we are is food for the worms, in the end I plan to bring some good stories to share with the dirt. I hope these four have a few good stories for the dirt.

"Chapter 8"

The four brothers, Hillbillies, whatever the fuck you want to call them made their way into their shack, cabin whatever. The four of them inside, I quickly make my way to their truck. I slide under the truck as if I were sliding into home plate for the winning score. I quickly take my blade and slice through the thick starter wire. I then cut their gas lines running from the gas tank to the engine, the same I had done to the previous brother's truck. I had no sooner done this and I was already back in the cornfield, under the cover of the cornstalks. I cover my entire body with fresh dirt as fast as I can. I had tried not to get any gas on my body at all but I was sure that at least a little had gotten on me. The dirt would cover the scent of the gasoline at least a little bit anyway.

I make my way away from my former hiding spot and to another not too far away. I am deep enough into the field I can easily hide, yet close enough to still have a great view of the cabin and the hillbillies. I knew that these fools would soon follow. I want them to follow the trail that I had left them leading to their brother. I was quick to cover any tracks leading to my current position. The reality was they would follow my trail into the field, yet that would be the biggest mistake of their soon to be short lives. Once in the field they would be in my world, the world of shadows and darkness, a world filled with death.

Cornfields always freaked me out in a way. When I was a kid back in Connecticut my grandfather forced me to watch Children of the Corn with him. Looking back I would say having an eight year old watch this movie was a pretty damn bad thing to do. Yet forcing an eight year old who would soon be moving to Nebraska, a land filled with cornfields was just fucking cruel. By the time I had made it to Iowa I was scared shit less. All I saw on both sides of the interstate were cornfields, with stalks that may have well as been twenty feet tall in my eyes. Now this may not sound that bad, yet in my head all I could do was wait for Malakai to come rushing from one of the fields and drag me in with him. Yet I also knew that he would only do this after killing my parents. I truly believed that I would end up one of those kids living out in the fields having to kill random passing strangers. I tried to close my eyes all the way through Iowa, only wishing that I could simply fall asleep. Yet once in Nebraska it was no different, only the occasional bean field broke up the corn fields. I seriously believe that I was scared the entire first month that I lived in Nebraska. Yet now laying on the ground deep within this field all I can really think is that I miss my Grandfather.

The four brothers all came running out of the cabin. The big fella is all hunched over holding his belly vomiting his guts out. I laugh to myself, this fucking bastard can kill innocent people, gut them like livestock, even eat them later and here he is vomiting at the sight of his dead brother. Fucking pussy, this display of weakness only makes me look forward to killing him more. Weakness can only be rewarded with pain, one must feel weakness in the flesh so they never forget its sting. Once one knows pain, once one has had their weakness imprinted into their flesh, only then will it never be forgotten. Weakness is a lesson one must learn, must learn through pain.

The little short fucker is crying like a bitch, screaming, why God, why God, why God, over and over again while holding his face in his palms. I am confused, why the hell would this fool even ask such a foolish question of God? Why would this fools little brother be killed? Let me think, I dint know maybe because he was a rapist fuck? Maybe because he was field dressing a woman like a damn deer getting ready to cook and eat her? I don't know those seem like a few reasons that may warrant a violent death in my eyes. I want to kill this little faggot right here and now just to calm my own anger. I catch myself, anger, anger will always get you killed, no emotion, emotions get you

killed. Anger coupled with emotions lead to rash
decisions, lead to mistakes, mistakes get you
killed. No anger here, just revenge, this is
just another mission. Only this mission has been
given to me by god, not some asshole sitting in
an office back in the Pentagon.

Only God could have given me this mission.
You see God knew that I needed a mission, a
reason to live again. You see when a coward ask
God to be strong, to be brave, God will never
snap his fingers and make you strong or make you
brave. No God does not work that way at all,
that would just be too damn simple, what would
you learn? No God will take that same man and
put him into a situation where he must be brave,
he must be strong. Then it is all up to you, did
you see the signs, did you receive Gods message?
Did you step up and be brave, be strong, as you

longed to do? Did you be the man that you were born to be? God gave you the choice, God gave you a gift, you chose the path. That is the trick, the way of God, God will give you exactly what you ask for, only he leaves it up to you to realize he is giving you your gift. I asked God why I am I here with a pistol in my mouth far more times that I care to even mention. God put me in the car with Jill, God allowed me to get so fucked up I was able to be taken prisoner. God made me watch Jill be killed in such a horrific way. All these things were a gift from God. God gave me a purpose again. God led me here to kill these sick fucks, to ensure that no one else will ever be killed or hurt by them again. What comes after I do not know, nor do I care, I will let God lead my way. No man can argue with his fate.

The brother who is around five foot ten looked out to the field and began screaming.

"I'm going to kill you, I am going to kill you, you God damn son of a bitch!!!I am going to fucking kill you!!"

I could see that his eyes were all red, welled up with tears. Anger, his first mistake and possibly his greatest mistake. I smiled it was going to be comical watching this fool bumble his way around trying to catch me. I am going to play with him, play with him even more than the other brothers. Soon they will all know they were going to die, all welcome their deaths, this fool, this fool would learn this lesson most of all.

The last of the brothers, the medium sized one I am calling him Princess looked terrified.

He ran straight to the truck and tried to start it, wanting nothing more than to make his escape. Not even a click, there was no way for them to fix that starter. The poor fool jumped out of the truck and noticed all of the gas on the ground. I had cut the line on four places making sure they could not fix it at all. I should have popped a tire but in my haste I forgot. My mistake, if I am ever in a situation like this one again I will remember to do so next time. I looked at the front plate on the truck, the first indication as to just where the hell I actually am. The plate read 53-A463. This is important due to the fact that in Nebraska each county has an assigned number to indicate that county. Fifty three on the license plate meant that I am in Stanton County, which meant as long as I was anyplace near where they plate read I was pretty close to Norfolk. As well if I am in Stanton County odds are I am no more than a half hour drive from home or thirty miles or so. I could easily walk that distance hiding in the fields. For just a moment I thought I could just get the hell out of there and make my way home. If I hitch hiked I knew I would be home in less than an hour.

It would be so damn easy, simply get the fuck out of here and get home. I can see the sun setting, I know Wayne would be east of here. If I do this though how many more people will die? I am obligated to kill these bastards, this is a mission from God, my moment to not be a coward. There comes a point in every man's life that he must give something back. I have done so much wrong, so many bad things, hurt and killed so many people, it pains me to admit, even to myself. I know that killing these fools will not atone for my sins, nor should it. One cannot barter or buy their way into heaven, just ask Constantine. They say follow God and his footprints, let go let God, all that shit I am not sure the exact saying. The point of the saying as I got it is that God does not give you more than you can handle. Well I do not know about all of that, to be honest I don't even care. My reality is well let's say skewed. I have seen so much horror, so much death, I have killed so many people that if there is a God, well fuck him! One day I hope to stand before him with a raised fist and simply yell, what the fuck you goddamn son of a bitch! Then with a great smile I will spit right in his face and tell him to send me to hell with all of my friends and family. Fuck that whole bad things happen to good people bullshit. Maybe I am not doing God's work by killing these fools at all? Maybe I am here to do the Devils work, well then fuck them both. In truth I am here to clean up a mistake made by both God and the Devil, a simple tool. You want the honest truth, I enjoy killing, I get off on torturing people, this shit gets my dick hard, and I love it when my dick is hard. Fuck it, I am a bad person, I am evil, and I am here to do my own work, not God's nor the devils.

So here is what is going to happen, there will be no act of God, nor, will there be any act of the Devil. No just the actions of a lone man who enjoys the reality that he is a demon, yet no better or worse than any other man. The ability to be like me is in us all, just so few of you allow it to surface. That is why you are weak and I am strong, I accept every aspect of my being. I am going to hunt and kill each one of these fuckers. I will torture them, make them beg me for death long before I allow them the luxury of dying. Finally after I have killed these men I will hit the road, possibly wondering killing those I deem as needing to die. That is my mission, fuck God and Fuck the Devil, I am God I am the Devil, only I will live like a hobo, invisible to the world, always hiding in plain sight.

"Chapter 9"

From my position in the field I could clearly hear the brothers talking.

"Did you see what that son of a bitch did?"

The medium sized one said to his brothers?

"He cut his fucking dick off and shoved it in his mouth, who the fuck does something like that?"

The big one cried out.

"We have to find him, where the fuck is Tommy."

One of the brothers damn near screamed? The smallest of the brother had been walking in circles.

"Hey guys look at this trail."

He told the others looking at the obvious trail I had left for them. The group of brothers were only feet from me now. I could easily shoot them all with the forty five I had taken, get this all over with fast, yet where would the fun be in that? I was invisible to them, a ghost. I could smell their fear. Fear, once your enemy fears you, then you control them. These fucks fear, these fucks fear is so thick in the air I could cut it with a knife.

"Look guys we have to follow this trail. I am sure that Tommy chased him in here and probably already killed the fucker."

The big fella told everyone.

"The fuck he did, you saw what this son of a bitch did to little Ryan."

The medium sized one said.

"We have to find this fucker and find Tommy. If we don't get to this guy he will go to the law and then we are really fucked."

"I don't know man, I don't think this guy is going to the law."

The little guy said.

"Yeah well if he does are you ready to spend the rest of your life in prison? Do you want some big fucking nigger fucking you in your ass and calling you cupcake, because I sure as fuck don't!!"

The big fella screamed!

"We have to get this guy, no if's ands or buts about it, do you fucking get it?"

He yelled at his brothers.

This is perfect for me I thought, I already know who their leader is. I guess that he must have been the one to kick the others asses when they were all kids. The big fucker will be my

next target. That old saying is an ancient one
and still true to this day, cut off the head of
the snake and you kill the body. The moment that
I kill this fucker the others will fall into a
panic. Once in a panic they will be even easier
for the picking. I have plans for them, each one
to see his brother's death, each one to know
they are next. Each one of them will know death
is coming for them, know pain, most of all know
terror. I will destroy their minds long before I
destroy their bodies.

Earlier I told you that I am not doing God
or the Devils work. As I see it I am still not
doing so. Yet like I told you in life we must
all atone for our previous sins, be it in this
life or the next. Now I have seen plenty of shit
that I will not or even attempt to try and
explain. Yet I am a logical man, I base

everything that I do off of compassion as well as evidence, that is my reality. I have no proof of an afterlife what so ever. I want to believe, yet without proof I am always left with more questions than answers. All that I know is the here and the now, what I can feel, I can taste, and I can touch. Who knows maybe this is all some Matrix type shit? Maybe this is all an illusion, who cares, this illusion is what I know to be real. The evidence that I have before me is that these bastards are rapist and cannibals. These men want to hunt me down and kill me. If I do not kill these men how many more people will they hurt or kill? How many more have to die? I am fates messenger, sent here to make these men atone for their actions, while I atone for my own. If they have to answer in the next life as well then so be it, here they will answer to me.

I looked at the brothers seeing the fear in their eyes.

"Come on you fucking pussies."

The big fella said as the brothers entered the field in a single file line.

"Man this trail is almost too damn good."

One of the brothers called out to his companions.

"It looks to me that something was dragged down through here."

The medium one said.

"Well let's just hope that it wasn't Tommy."

The big one called out.

"You think that Tommy made it?

The little one asked?

"I don't know man."

One of the brothers said.

"Tommy, Tommy!"

The big fella called out at the top of his lungs. The medium one looked at his larger brother.

"Shut the fuck up man! You are letting this psycho know exactly where we are at yelling like that."

"You stupid little bitch!"

The big fella said as he grabbed his brother by the front of his shirt.

"You think that this mother fucker doesn't already know where we are? Don't you ever tell me what to do again you little bitch or you won't have to worry about any mother fucker hiding in the fields. You got that you little bitch?"

"Fuck you asshole, don't think because you are bigger than me I won't kick your ass."

The medium size one told his larger brother.

"After we are done hunting this mother fucker down like a dog, I plan to gut him and cook him in a pit."

The medium size one said.

"When we are done with this task, I will be kicking your ass for that bitch remark."

"Well little brother until then you are in this hot ass field with me getting cut up by these cornstalks, but don't get your shit twisted we will be talking later."

The big fella told his smaller brother.

It's hot, near ninety degrees with just as high of a dew point, even hotter in the fields. Nebraska, what a fucked up place for weather. The winters here are like forty below zero wind chills, so damn cold that often you will look at the temps in Nebraska and it will be warmer in fucking Alaska. The spring times here are filled with rain and tornadoes. The only real nice time of the year is fall and that is filled mainly with watching football on TV rather than being outdoors. The best part of fall is all of the hunting. You get to go pheasant hunting, I so love pheasant hunting, hell hunting in general.

Right now hunting is exactly what I am doing.

Only rather than hunting pheasant I am hunting

people. Did you ever really think that being a

sniper was anything different than hunting? As a

sniper I was trained to hunt at the highest

level, hunting the of beast the world's greatest

target, man. People are targets, no different

than a deer or an elk. Truth be told I have more

emotion for a deer that I kill than I do a man.

I believe that this is due to the fact that a

deer is my food, it will nourish me, keep me

alive. My targets, my targets are all takers,

users, people that this world will be better off

without.

I watch the brothers from a distance, yet

still very close to them. The key is to move

with your targets so as not to make any out of

place movements. I could easily get in front of these idiots and take the big one out with my spear if I chose to. No not yet, he needed to see his other brother first, he needed to see that death would soon come to him as well.

"Were almost down by the creek."

I hear one of the brothers called out.

"Look up there the hawks are circling, they must see something down in the creek."

The little one called out.

"Well I don't care if there is a dead deer down there or not I am about to jump in that damn creek and take a swim.

The big fella called out laughing. I tried to hold back my laughter at his remark. I was close enough he would hear me if I did so. I totally understood where he was coming from with this damn heat. Unlike them I at least had water that I could drink to cool me off. Not to mention that I was still covered in mud keeping my body cool and keeping it from getting burnt. I could already see the brothers beginning to pink up already.

I learned to ignore weather during my military training. We were all taught to ignore cold, to ignore heat, ignore rain, ignore snow, all weather is just that, weather. Only the target and the mission matter. I worked out of so many countries, so many climates, none mattered to me. Shit, in one week I pulled a mission in Africa only to be on a glacier by the end of that week. Normal people can't deal with shit like that, hell I shouldn't be able to cope with shit like that, but I can. I guess one of the benefits of growing up in a bipolar climate like North East Nebraska. The only difference between you and I is that I am trained to block it all out. Out of sight out of mind, mind over matter that's all. Right now these brothers are all drenched in sweat, starting to burn, longing for a drink of water, me, well I am just fine.

I am close enough that I can smell their sweat. They all stink of cheap liquor and bad diets. Only the little fella doesn't wreak of booze or meth, just a horrible body odor. They are all stumbling now, I take it that they don't get a lot of exercise. I am tired as well, yet I must work my way through it, once again all a state of mind.

"Hey what the fuck is that?"

The big brother screams. He jumps down the bank of the creek sliding on his ass down the dirt embankment. It looks to me as if it hurts him, these dirt clods can be no damn joke. The brothers all get to the edge of the bank and take in the sight that drove their brother to leap down the creek embankment.

"No, fuck, fuck, fuck!"

The medium size brother screams out.

The brothers all make their way down the creek bank to the creek bed.

"Tommy, Tommy, what the fuck man? Look at him, fucking look at him!"

The medium size brother screamed!

"Who the fuck, what the fuck does this, God fucking damn it! Fuck you, Fuck you, you god

damn son of a bitch, I am going to fucking kill
you!"

The medium sized brother screams! The other
two brothers are on their knees crying at the
feet of their dead brother, the whole sight is
really comical to me.

Looking down on Tommy I could see that the
animals had all made quick work of his remains.
A large chunk of his entrails had been devoured
by the animals. A bunch of the animals had
actually severed chunks of the entrails, there
were random piles of guts on the bank as well as
floating in the water. The sickest yet coolest
part of the whole thing was what the birds had
done to the body. I could see that that the
hawks had already plucked out Tommy's eyes,
along with half of his face. The flies were

everywhere, it looked as if there was a dark cloud around the body. Most would see this as some disgusting shit, not me, to me it is a return to the earth. The reality is that this is actually how it is supposed to be. I watched the brothers around their brother. I couldn't help but think that if they had any sort of heart they would cut their brother down from his makeshift cross and let his body float to the bottom of the natural pool in the creek.

"Chapter 10"

"What the fuck are we supposed to do goddamn it?"

One of the brothers screamed out.

"Cut Tommy down we can't leave him like that."

The big fella told his brothers.

"What the fuck is the point?"

The smallest of the brothers said.

"Seriously there is no god damn way that we could ever explain this shit to anyone. On the real you guys know that every death is investigated, how the hell would this get explained, tell me that god damn it."

The little one screamed out to his brothers.

"No he is right if we report any of this shit we are all fucked."

The medium sized brother told the group.

"So what the fuck do you pussies think we should do, leave Tommy up there to be eaten by the fucking animals?"

The big fella called out.

"He deserves to be buried."

"So what the worms can eat him?"

The little one asked?

"So what then genius, what do we do with him?"

The big fella asked?

"I say that we cut him down and push him into the pool, let his body sink down into the deepest part of the creek. We all know that he wouldn't want no Christian burial nor would he want to be worm food. I say let the catfish he loved to fish take care of his remains, it's kind of fitting anyway."

The medium sized brother told the group.

"Well then, what about little Ryan and the whore?"

"I say we throw them into the creek as well."

"Dude you are fucking heartless."

The brother between the medium size and small brother who usually kept quiet piped up.

"No bro I am being realistic here, if any of this gets reported or found out we will all be in prison. I am also pretty damn sure that none of us would ever be getting out either."

"No as fucked up as it sounds Sean is right."

The big fella said.

"There isn't shit that we can do here, I mean nothing. Believe me if there was I would say that we do it, but as far as I see it we are all out of options here."

The smaller brother called out to the group.

"This shit isn't Christian at all."

The normally quiet brother called out.

"Christian, are you fucking kidding me? Do you think anything that we do is fucking Christian?"

The larger of the brothers asked almost sounding disgusted?

"Brother I assure you if there is a heaven or a hell after we leave this world I highly suggest you get your shorts and some fucking sunscreen out because you are for sure going to fucking hell. How fucking stupid are you? We fucking kidnap people, we rape women and men, we kill people, then to top it all off we fucking eat them. Now please you fucking retard, tell me what part of any of that shit sounds fucking Christian or God fearing to you?

Now get the fuck out of my face you little faggot bitch"

The big fella said as he cut down his dead brother from his makeshift cross.

"Well big brother I hope that in death that you find all that you couldn't in life."

The big fella said as he pushed his brother's body or what was left of it into the deep water pool. I sat in my hide, watching and listening to everything the brothers were doing. The body took on water fast due to the belly having been opened. I could tell that the two medium sized brothers were not happy with this at all. I watched intently as the body slipped under the milk chocolate brown water. The brothers were crying, with the normally quiet one making the sign of the cross and seemingly praying. Prayer, the last refuge of a desperate man.

"So what now?"

The small brother asked the big fella?

"We get Ryan and the whore and throw them into the creek as well."

"What about the crazy fucker?"

"I would lay good money that he is gone by now, there are four of us and I am sure knowing we were down here he used it as his time to escape."

The big fella said.

"You sure about that bro?"

"Would you stick around man?"

"Hell no I would get the fuck out of Dodge."

"Exactly little brother that is why I am sure that he is gone. Don't worry he is far from the area by now, and after what he did he can't go to the cops either. Don't worry the car had

Wayne County plates, he is from the area we will find him soon enough and take care of him then, cool little brother?"

"Yeah I can live with that, we will get this son of a bitch soon enough."

Get me soon enough, please. I am sure that shit sounded really good in their heads. Get me, I was long gone, little did these fuckers know that I was less than twenty feet away from them at all times. I have always loved the bullshit that people will tell themselves to feel better. I used to be like that, hell we all have at one point. Yet there comes a day for us all that we have to stand in front of the mirror naked and just look at ourselves. You can't lie to yourself when you're staring at your own body naked in the mirror. No, life will come full circle on your ass at that point. Life fucking sucks when we lie to ourselves. I have always loved the old analogy that life is like getting to take a whore on a date. You take a whore out who would have given you the pussy with no real work, yet you fucked up, you took her on a date. Now this normally easy piece of ass that has already fucked two counties feels special and guess what, feeling like a good woman, you don't get any pussy. Moral of the story, life is never certain, at any moment all you have ever known to be true can flip upside down on you.

I kept my position, hidden in the brush I listen to and watch my prey.

"I will stay here and keep guard."

The big fella told his brothers.

"Yeah, keep guard fuck you man, I still think that fucker is out there."

The little guy said.

"Look I am going to make sure Tommy's body don't float up or wind up in the shallow part of the creek, you guys go get Ryan and the fucking whore. Anyway, do feel safer dip shit with three of your brothers or alone here?"

He scoffed truly believing that I had fled in his mind.

"You sure that you are cool here alone man?"

The medium size brother asked?

"I already told you pussies that fucker is damn near to Wayne by now, let's get this damn shit taken care of before the damn law shows up.

Look you idiots if that fucker says anything to anyone and he still may the pigs will be here in a second, so we don't have much time to clean this shit up. As far as I see it we will even have to burn the cabin down."

"Really you think so?"

The medium size brother asked.

"Hell yeah I do you have watched all the cop shows with me, those pigs got so much technological shit that they can see blood from twenty damn years ago now days."

The big fella said almost pissed off sounding that his brother would even doubt him.

"We can't leave any evidence at all man, in fact I even plan on leaving town for a while. I will not spend the rest of my life locked up in a damn cage. I have seen how those fuckers all live on Lock Up Raw and that is no life for me."

The big fella said almost looking like he had tears in his eyes.

"I will not end up in prison and neither will you guys if I can help it."

"No bro, no bro, you are right as always."

The medium size brother said clearly seeing the fear and frustration in his brother's eyes.

"We are going now to get the bodies we will be back as fast as we can."

I watched from my hide as all four of the brothers made their way up the creek bank. From my position I could watch the entire field. Ten to fifteen minuet's each way, another fifteen plus to round up the bodies, and that was if they moved with haste. The fact that one of the bodies was the dismembered body of their baby brother may just add another ten minuet's to the time, perfect. I figured that this would give me at least forty five minutes till the brothers returned. Knowing that a few of the brothers doubted that I had actually taken off meant that they would move with as much haste as possible. All I needed was the right moment to strike. The key is patience, I didn't want to have to fight this big fucker, I know that I can take him, yet I am man enough to admit that I may get my ass kicked a bit and possibly hurt in the process. Patience, back in sniper school we learned patience over all else. A hunter can never rush, yet patient or not I did not have a lot of time here. Leaving him alone was a gift to me. I was left to wonder if the big fella didn't stay knowing I was here, longing for death out of his own guilt. Staying alone was almost inviting death in my eyes, like Luis with Le stat in Interview with the Vampire. Fuck it, his motives don't matter to me, all that matters to me is taking his life.

I sat watching the big fella, studying my prey like any true hunter would do. I could tell that he was frantic, scared, he was so far out of his comfort zone or element if you will. It was him who hunted and harmed people, him who drove fear into others, not the other way around. Fear, fear breeds mistakes. Fear coupled with stupidity allowed his greatest mistake, staying here alone. Everyone knows that the lion always takes the animal on the edge of the heard.

The big fella was sitting down, his face buried in his hands. I could hear him crying.

"Why, why, why, why my brothers, this isn't fair God."

Blaming God, the total last refuge of a desperate man. I began to inch closer and closer to the big fucker. In my hand I held the very knife that had been used to disembowel my poor friend Kim. I am moving silently in the tall weeds and native grass along the ridge. I could hear the big fucker.

"Why God, he was just a boy. He was just a boy God, why, why, why?"

I laughed to myself, just a boy, just a rapist, just a murderer, just a fucking cannibal, that boy deserved to die, needed to die. How many had met their demise at the hands of these fuckers, how many raped and tortured? I am fates messenger, I am a tool of the Gods, here to deliver evil to hell.

The good don't die young, they just haven't had enough time to fuck up like the rest of us is all. That boy deserved to die. More so, I was happy to kill him. I would gladly kill that little fucker over and over again simply for the joy of doing so. I am mere feet away from the big fucker, still crying like a little bitch. Maybe at this moment he was having his first moment with God, good, soon I will allow him to meet the creator he has just come to. I can smell his sweat, as I told you before a foul body odor mixed with booze and bad dietary choices. I could see his back expand with each inhalation, hear his sobs. I am not two feet from my prey now.

I am reminded of a kill I made back in Afghanistan. I was in the mountains for two damn weeks tracking, waiting for just the right moment to make my move. My target was a high ranking member of Al Quida. I stalked him for weeks, never once being discovered, always mere feet away from him. Finally I got my moment right as he got done taking a shit. I am a good man, I allowed him to take his last shit. I could have taken him out before, yet I allowed him that one last male luxury. You see enemy soldier or not, he was still a man in my eyes. I have never held malice or anger towards any of my targets until now. He believed that his side of the war was right, I didn't care if my side was right or wrong. I was just there to do a job, and my job was to kill my target. I let him take his last shit. Then just as he opened the door I got him, cutting his throat before he could make a sound. I pushed him back into the shitter then pushed my blade down into his heart. I left him in the shitter, I doubt that anyone checked on him for near an hour, allowing me all the time that I needed to get the hell out of there and to my extraction point.

Today I hold malice towards my targets. I feel sad, I do not have the time to properly torture this big fucker before his brother's return. My prey still has his hands covering his face. I guess he is still trying to figure out what the hell has just happened over the last fifteen hours or so, poor fool. I leap from my position, the big fucker jumps up startled. I smash him with the handle of the blade in the side of his temple. I leap up Thai fighter style and smash his jaw with my knee, knocking the big son of a bitch out cold. I quickly rip off his shirt and use it to secure his hands and feet. My victim began to come to trying to speak and yell but his broken jaw didn't allow him to do so.

"Well hey there you big fucker seems as though shit has gone a bit sideways here for you. I thought it was you that had all of the heart out of your fucked up group of inbred brothers. I have watched you cry like a bitch for the last ten minutes, pretty pathetic man."

"I'm sorry, I'm sorry."

He tried to say through his broken jaw.

"Well big man I hate to tell you this but sorry just doesn't fucking cut it with me man. I personally believe that we were meant to meet this way. I know that God lead me to you, and

God wants me to kill you and your entire family. This whole fucked up situation has been a blessing really, we are both part of a divine path big man, do you understand me?"

"Don't kill me, don't kill, please don't kill me."

"Man I expected so much more out of you big man, I mean fuck look at the size of your big ass."

I place my hand on the big man's forehead.

"Big man, I am not sorry for what I am about to do to you. Believe me if we had more time I would do things to you that Satan himself would look away from."

I said as I ruffled his greasy hair.

"Well big man I hope that you enjoy this."

I said as I pushed down on big man's face cutting with my knife along the bone structure of the face. Big man wanted to scream but couldn't. My cuts deep enough I slipped my blade under the skin, making a pocket of you will. Blood is pouring from big man's face, whenever you cut the face it bleeds like a stuck pig. The whole creek is turning red from big man's blood running into it. I dig my fingers into the pockets that I had created and began pulling the face from the skull. As big man's face peels from the bone it makes a kind of squishing noise mixed with a slight crunching sound. I had never done this to a human before, I was just doing what I had done to animals when I butchered them. Now that I have done this I do have to say it's really no different than doing this to a deer.

After pulling the face from the skull all of the muscles and tendons were now exposed. I hate to say this but it looked just like a scene from Hell-Raiser the movie. Either they had really good make up people or they killed some people, the shit looked dope. Happy with my work I placed the face in my pocket for later use. The big fucker was writhing in agony, well past the point of being able to scream.

"Well big fucker I hate the fact that you didn't put up any sort of a fight. Maybe my expectations were just too damn high with you. I really did think that you would have a bit more heart, but the size of the man doesn't always dictate the size of the fight in a man I guess. Well should we end this man?"

I took big man's face from my pocket and put it over my own.

"Look at me fucker!"

I said as I grabbed him.

"Look at me bitch!"

I said as I pushed my blade deep inside of his belly, his eyes fixed on mine wearing his face like a mask. I pulled my blade from the wound and reached up inside of the big man like an ancient Mayan priest and grabbed big man's heart. I could feel it beating so fast it was as if he was running a marathon. I grabbed the heart as tight as I could and gave it a huge tug ripping it free from the arteries holding it in place. I pulled the heart free of the big fucker's body. Holding the heart over my head I allowed the blood to pour over my body. I have no real clue as to why I am doing this at all. I am holding the heart in front of me now, I take a huge bite out of it ripping a chunk free with my teeth, my first taste of human flesh. I could taste the salty blood covering my entire mouth. I swallow the chuck of heart feeling it the entire way down to my stomach.

I place the heart in big man's mouth. I take big man's face off of mine and place it back in my pocket and make my way back to my hide. I know that the others will be returning soon with the bodies of Jill and that little rat boy. I wanted to know I needed to see their faces when they all saw their big brother. I had a gift for them all, their brothers face.

"Chapter 11"

     I ran full tilt and made my way to a
perfect hide just at the edge of the creek where
the drop off and field meet. I began covering
myself with more dirt which quickly turned to
mud from the blood covering my body. I laughed,
that big fella bled a lot. When I cut open his
stomach cavity his blood damn near sprayed all
over me. I have realized over the years that
fear mixed with high blood pressure means that
your victim's blood will spray from their body
like a fountain. I looked down at the big
fucker's body laying at the edge of the creek. I
could already see some craw fish not only
climbing on but into the big fella's body

through the opening in the belly that I had
made.

I am rather surprised at just how long the
brothers are taking getting back. For a moment
the reality that they may have just said fuck it
and fuck their brother and split hits my mind.
Wouldn't that be fucked up, this pack of
inbreeds ditching their own brother, using him
as their sacrificial lamb. I told you earlier,
once fear sets in you are fucked, the mind no
longer works properly. Fear is like a fast
moving cancer. Once fear gets into your body it
begins to spread all throughout one's soul. The
mind begins to rush as fast as the heart does.
Once this begins to happen you make rash
decisions, bad decisions, decisions that will
easily get you killed. Fear had sunk into the
very soul of the big man. So much fear entered

him that he broke down and cried, simply gave
up, gave in to allowing death to come to him.
Before he died the big man hit rock bottom, his
lowest point.

We all hit rock bottom at one point in our
short lives at least once or twice. I remember
the first time in my life that I hit rock
bottom. I was in my car, I had no money, illegal
plates, as well as warrants out for my arrest.
My wife had kicked me out of our home for
reasons that I wasn't even sure of. Plain and
simple I was in my car, homeless, knowing that
if I were to get arrested that would be the best
possible thing for me. If I went to jail I would
have a roof over my head, a place to sleep, as
well as three meals a day be they shitty ones or
not. Most of all I would have time to think,
time to decide upon my next move.

A single tear began to find its way down my cheek, followed by a flood of tears. I was at my rock bottom. Whenever jail is your best possible option, well my friend you are at your lowest point. Then it hit me like a Mack truck. For the first time in my life I was exactly where I was supposed to be. Once you hit rock bottom if you are able to actually realize it you have just found your way to one of the greatest moments of your life. Each step that I took from that moment forward would be a step forward, a step up. A shitty apartment was a step up from the back seat of my car. Even the smallest step forward was a leap for me. My agony all turned to utter joy. That moment helped to define the rest of my life thus far, and since then I have never looked back.

I later realized that it wasn't easy for my former wife to live with a man who killed people for a living. As well it wasn't easy for her to be with a man who was rarely there. Each night that I was gone she later told me she would cry wondering if I were alive or dead. She had no clue what shit hole country I was in. she always feared that I was someplace being held prisoner, being tortured to death. She also felt as though I brought home with me the ghost of all those that I would kill. In hind sight I can't blame her, I would be a fool to do so.

Even when we were together I realize now that I was cold and distant, lost almost. I couldn't tell her about the things that I had did, the ghost haunting me, even if that was my only desire. I knew that not only would she ever understand why I had done the things that I had done, but would have truly seen the monster that I had become. I wasn't that same boy she had met in that trailer so many years before. I had grown, evolved into a stone cold killer, a killer who enjoyed his work. I could never relate to her world, nor she to mine. How could I ever pretend to understand some office drama bull shit? I would try to pretend, but she could tell I was only pretending. Looking back I am glad that she kicked me out of her life. To be honest looking back I know now that there was nothing positive that I could have brought to her life. I also thank her, I thank her for forcing me to rock bottom, dragging me down to my lowest point, allowing me to experience the greatest moment of my life.

I closed my eyes and simply listened to the nature around me. I took an old Buddhist tip,

live in this moment, this moment is all that
exist. Disregarding my own advice I allowed my
mind to drift to years past. A woman that I
loved named Elizabeth popped into my thoughts,
damn did I hurt that poor girl. All Elizabeth
ever wanted was to be loved. If I could have
loved her even half as much as she loved me she
would have been happy. I was going through so
many things at the time. By things I was dealing
with a lot of demons.

Far too often you end up doing what you
have to do deal with your personal demons,
regardless of whether you hurt others. It's
scary really, all those faces that you have
thrown in the fuck it bucket climbing out
showing themselves. The ghost of the past are
often far too real. I understand not only how
but why so many former soldiers take their own

lives. You are bred, made into a fighting dog, made into a cold hearted killer. You become hard as steel, not only physically but mentally. You are trained that no matter what you do, no matter how fucked up, you simply throw it in the fuck it bucket. The fuck it bucket, mine is overflowing, I am sorry Elizabeth.

I tried to love her as she deserved, I just couldn't. That old saying is true, you can't love someone if you can't love yourself. I never once hit her with my hands, no I did far worse. I beat Elizabeth day in and day out with my words. My actions made her not only question us, but herself. I was a toxic poison in her life, yet she still loved me. She would have done anything for me had I only let her.

Elizabeth's last straw was her catching me cheating on her. I didn't even try to hide what I had done. I couldn't have hidden my actions even if I wanted to. Doing what only one of the biggest assholes in life could ever do to a woman, I slept with her best friend. I could have blamed her, blamed the booze, blamed the weed, but that would have all been a lie. I was just an asshole, I saw pussy, I went after it, and I fucked it, plain and simple.

In hind sight I would take it all back if I could, at least at one point I would have. Now I see it as the girl was simply fate, it took me getting caught fucking that girl for Elizabeth to be able to move on. I was just like every other piece of shit asshole out there, I saw pussy I fucked it, I thought only with my dick. Men are not as strong as women with regards to cheating. As a man we know we should listen to our hearts, yet in the heat of the moment our hearts are whispering to us, the whole while our dicks are screaming at us. I heard a while back that Elizabeth was married now. I even heard that she has three kids now. Elizabeth is living down in Omaha now working as an insurance salesperson. I am happy for her, I hope that she has not only found but is living the life that I could never have given her, the life that she deserves. I hope the same for every woman that I have ever hurt.

"Chapter 12"

I opened my eyes, still listening to everything going on around me. Even while lost in old memories my senses were always active to the world around me. I could hear rustling in the field, the sounds of footsteps. Next came the voices, these fools had no clue with regards to the concept of stealth. Any sniper or Special Forces officer would not only hear them but smell them from a mile away. These dip shits wouldn't last ten minuet's in any sort of a battle situation. I had expected that their years of hunting would have taught them something, but I guess not. I am sitting silent, covered in mud and brush, I am invisible.

"Damn this bitch is heavy."

The larger of the two medium size brothers said as he held Jill's feet.

"Yeah well for only being twelve years old Ryan isn't to light here himself."

The smaller brother called out.

"This shit is so damn fucked up, let's just get this shit done and get the fuck out of here guys."

The smallest of the brothers said.

"I can't believe that shit went this damn sideways."

The medium size brother said.

"How many damn times have we done this before? Nothing like this has ever happened to us, I just can't get my head around it."

"What the fuck are you even saying right now, you know as well as me that it was only a matter of time before something went wrong."

The larger of the medium size brothers says.

"The shit that we have been doing is wrong, it is beyond wrong, do you all really think that God was going to let us get away with this shit forever."

The smallest of the brothers said.

"No little brother you are right, we should have never let Tommy get us into all of this shit. Fuck we were all just kid's man, we were never even given a chance."

"Yeah well we are here now and it is what it is so let's just get this shit done and get our asses whey the fuck out of here."

The largest of the group said.

He was right, it is what it is. The reality is that they had all gone way too far to turn back. I myself am far from innocent, even I had traveled way past the point of turning back long ago. I hadn't only knocked on the Devil's door I kicked that shit in with an M4 in my hand rock and rolling the room. Life often takes us places that we never expected at all. It is up to us to do what it is that we do when the moment arises, not fate. The hard part is excepting what we have done after we have done it. Me, I just went with the force, became one with the moment. I have never really believed in anything but the moment anyway. The past, well the past no longer exist, the past is just there to have learned from. The future, well that shit doesn't exist either. No man is promised tomorrow, yet near one hundred percent of men believe that they are.

Most people waste each day, unsure if it really actually happened to be honest. They all say that they are living for the weekend. I have never thought of a more terrible existence than this. The whole idea that you only get to live for two single days a week is a pathetic existence at best. Yet despite all of these beliefs that I have, I am scared to die. Yes I the big bad soldier, the sniper with hundreds of confirmed kills, hell hundreds that are classified am afraid to die. Yet this is a good thing in my eyes. This fear of death keeps me sharp, keeps me in focus. A man that does not fear death is a fool or a damn liar. This man will always make mistakes, he is simply too damn cocky. No that man is not me, I relish my fear, I use my fear, most of all I respect my fear of death.

The brothers were almost at the edge of the creek. I looked down on their brothers body, a

hawk was tearing at the flesh of his face. I
could see that the hawk had already torn out the
eyes. I figured they must do this because it is
the softest part, the eyes must have a lot of
protein in them I thought. I have noticed that
birds of prey always go for the eyes and the
belly. Nature does everything for a reason, thus
these parts must have the highest amounts of
protein. Well, maybe it is just an easy place to
get at the meat, who knows. I don't know, I
guess it is just an observation that I have made
over the years. The hawk's talons were covered
in blood from ripping large chunks of meat from
the body. I have said this before, it is a
beautiful sight to see nature do its thing.

The brothers made their way to the creek,
calling out for their brother. Once at the edge

of the creek they looked down the bank and saw
what was left of their brother's body.

"What the fuck!!"

The bigger of the medium size brothers
yelled. The brothers dropped both Jill's body
and their little brothers body and ran down the
bank to their brother's corpse. The smallest of
the brothers tripped and rolled down the bank,
landing in the water of the creek. It was funny
watching him, if there had been snow on the
ground he would have been a snowball by the time
he hit the water.

"Ah fuck, my fucking leg!"

He screamed out holding his leg in pain. I
could tell even from the distance I was away
from him that his leg was broken. My senses
kicked in instantly, I am a lion on the plains

of Africa. This brother is now the wounded zebra on the edge of the heard.

"Look at his fucking face man."

One of the brothers screamed out.

"He cut off his fucking face man, what the fuck, why the hell did he do this?"

One of the brothers took his brothers heart from his mouth.

"Look at this shit, he took a fucking bite out of it man, he ate part of his goddamn heart."

"Yeah well that means that he is no better than us man."

The larger of the medium size brothers said.

"What the hell do we do now guys?"

The injured brother asked?

"I don't know?"

The larger of the medium size brothers called out now seemingly taking the role of the alpha.

Fear and confusion, I was already winning the battle. The truth is that I could leave these bastards alive and they would be looking over their shoulders for me for the rest of their lives. I would forever be their boogieman. I now held a greater spot in their hearts and souls more than anyone ever had in their lives. I am now the monster under the bed, the man whose very name you never say three times. When you have filled your enemies entire being with fear such as this you have already won.

The three brothers were all freaking out. This is my chance to turn shit up a little bit, I thought. I quickly ran through the field back to the cabin. I had an idea to instill even more fear into these guy's hearts. At a brisk walk it would take ten minuet's to get back to the cabin at a run I could do it in five. I could feel my heart pounding as I ran through the field. It had been far too long since I ran at all. I used to run five to ten miles every day. That was all before I began drinking all of the booze and doing all of the drugs. It felt good to feel my lungs burn a bit from running, I have missed this feeling. I ran through the trail made by the brothers, this was good. These fools had left a path two damn rows wide for me to run through. Best of all, the damn corn stalks were not slapping or cutting my face,

I remember my first year working in the corn fields pulling tassels, I was just fourteen years old. I had more cuts on my body than I ever had before in my life that year. Few realize that the green corn leaves can be as sharp as a razor if you hit it the wrong way. Thankfully the brothers made it sure that this wasn't going to be an issue for me. It seemed that it only took me an instant to be on the front porch of the cabin looking at the cabins front door. I quickly made my way into the cabin and drank as much water as I could. I also filled my bottles with water, I was sure that I would need them. It was still hot as fuck out and as always the humidity was horrific.

I quickly made my way back outside. Even if the brothers were on their way back there was no way that they would be here yet. I pulled the

big fuckers face from my pocket. I took my knife
and cut three small holes in in the face. I then
weaved the face through the holes of the trucks
antenna. I was sure to keep the holes tight so
no damn birds would come and carry the face
away. I stood looking at the big fuckers face
hanging on the trucks antenna. It took me back
to the mountains of Afghanistan back in two
thousand and four. I had begun taking the heads
of enemy troops. I would leave them on stakes as
calling cards for the enemy forces.

There is no damn Geneva Convention when you
are alone in the mountains of a war zone.
Everyone there wanted to kill me, and I in turn
wanted to kill everyone that I came across. The
heads, the heads made me a legend. I began not
only taking out my target but ten or twenty
others as well, whole troops sometimes. I was

told that I was known as a demon sent from hell. I was also told that there was a five hundred thousand dollar reward on my head. No one knew what I actually looked like, thus there was a five hundred thousand dollar reward on any American's head. We snipers were used to this, rewards on our heads just come with the job. Word had gotten back to the commanders about what I may or may not have done. Denial is the key, I simply said I had no clue as to what anyone was talking about. The brass knew that I was full of shit, but they couldn't afford to have shit like that hitting the press. It didn't matter, the reality was that I got the job done, I always got results. Despite this I never lost sight of the reality that results or not, I was always expendable, we all were.

"Chapter 13"

I came back to reality, I was gone for a second. Without the booze and the drugs to suppress the memories I seem to find myself trapped in a multi-dimensional existence. The booze and the drugs pushed all of the memories into that numb place, the fuck it region of my mind. Like the levies of New Orleans the fuck it bucket proved not to be strong enough to hold back the torrent. Not having booze and drugs to suppress all of these old memories, it is a good thing, I need to deal with my demons face to face.

I made my way back into the field, covered in mud hidden in the shadows. I sat in silence listening for the brothers. It felt good to feel

the wind beneath my arms and legs. If my hair
wasn't covered in mud I would have had the joy
of the breeze blowing through my hair. I made my
way back to the edge of the creek at a full but
silent run in what I estimated to be less than
five minutes. Not bad in my opinion for being so
out of damn shape. I hunkered down between the
rows of corn using the shadows to make myself
invisible. I looked up at the sun, no more than
an hour and it would be setting. Fucking
Nebraska in the summer the damn sun will stay up
till nine or ten o'clock at night. That is one
crazy thing about Nebraska in the summer, we
have some crazy long days, good for growing
crops though.

I could see the three remaining brothers
down at the creek bottom debating their next
moves. It made me sad to look over and see

Jill's body laying lifeless just feet from me. Her corpse barley look recognizable to me anymore, I remembered her so full of life, the glow was now gone. Jill's skin had turned a dark reddish kind of purple color now. I could tell that the blood had all coagulated in her veins. Not only that but she and the boy had really began to smell bad. Just looking at Jill made me want to shed a tear. How many nights had Jill and I spent together? Jill was a great person, she would always hold a place in my heart. Looking at her corpse I knew that wasn't Jill anymore, just her shell. To me Jill's corpse was just verification that what I was doing was right and that all these inbred fucks needed to die. It is up to me to make sure that these bastards never hurt anyone else again.

"So what the fuck are we going to do man?"

The smaller of the medium sized brothers asked his two brothers?

"I say fuck it lets just get the hell out of here."

The larger of the brothers said.

"I'm with you man."

The smallest brother, called out.

"I say we get the fuck out of here and head straight down to Cousin John's place down in bayou country down in Louisiana."

The smallest brother told the group.

"As far as I see it we can get lost down there. That is the type of place that few people ever ask any questions, especially if you already have kin down there."

"Fuck it let's do it."

The larger of the medium sized brother said.

"Let's get you to a hospital though first little brother and get that leg fixed."

I could see that his leg was already red and very swollen.

"What about the bodies?"

The larger of the brothers asked?

"Fuck them, roll them into the water and let the animals take care of them."

The new alpha told his brothers.

"Come on fuck this shit let's get the hell out of here."

He told his two brothers.

I watched in silence watching the two brothers try and help their injured brother up the creek embankment. On the real I am almost impressed with their team work. There was many a time that I had to help a fallen or injured brother out of danger. It is your duty to help a brother or a brother in arms. We were not simply put on this earth to work and die, no we were here for far greater things. I had already purchased my ticket to hell life time's ago. Others though, others must help as many as they can, it's too late for me but possibly not for them. My reality is that it is far too late for me, on the real, I am good with that.

I decided on my plan, a simple plan really, pick off the weakest link. That is what a lion would do, out here I am a lion. I love the hunt, I love the hunt even more that I do the kill.

The kill, well the actual kill is like blowing
your load, it's awesome, but short lived. I like
to think of the kill as trying to fuck some hot
ass girl. You have been pining for this woman,
dreaming about her, you put in all the work and
finally she lets you take her out. You put all
of your best moves on her and by the luck of the
Gods, or her boredom she decides to sleep with
you. Then the moment you get her clothes off you
begin to see all of her flaws, you had a perfect
image in your mind. Then she begins to give you
head, in your dreams she took it all the way
down to the balls, the reality is she barely
takes the head in her mouth and drags her teeth
on top of that. Then after you can't take no
more you finally push your cock into what you
thought was going to be the tightest pussy in
the world. Reality, this girl is loose as a damn

goose, you can't even aim for the sides. Now for the true kicker, she can't even move right, you push forward she moves with you rather than against you, it just plain sucks. You have to close your eyes and think of another woman just to bust a nut. Every man has had this happen, I am sure every woman in her way as well, luckily it happened to me back in high school, I learned young. To the point that is far too often what the kill is like. The hunt, the hunt is always better.

In this case though, well in this case I have enjoyed both the hunt and the kill, a rarity in this life. Normally I have no real reason at all to kill a man. For me they are all just targets, a face on a picture. This time the whole situation was personal. I have always enjoyed killing but never as much as I have today. While the circumstances are rather shitty I must admit it has been one hell of a fun day.

I hate to admit it but I realize that killing is all that I am really good at. I should that these inbred fucks for reminding me of my calling. I am sad that these bastards killed Jill, yet Jill did not die in vain, no Jill died for me. It was Jill's death that led me to these bastards. The Gods themselves took Jill here for the sole purpose of leading me to my mission, to my calling. This has all been the work of the Gods, Jill, me, just simple pawns. We are all simple playthings of the Gods, tools if we are lucky. I am a tool of the Gods, a simple hammer, a simple saw, here to clean up the gods mess.

"Chapter 14"

     The brothers took about ten minuet's to get

their smaller brother up the creek embankment.

If they would have been in a battle situation

team work or not they would have all been dead.

I am sitting in silence, invisible, only three

rows of corn away from the brothers. It is

almost funny to me that they cannot see me at

all. The rows of corn are near six and a half

feet tall. The corn blocks out the sunlight

leaving only shadows and random beams of light

cutting through the darkness, dancing with the

breeze. For a split second I remembered being a

kid again, fearing the corn fields after being

tortured by my grandfather with that damn

Children of the Corn movie. God I believed for

years that the corn children were going to
kidnap me and make me a sacrifice to their corn
god.

I listened to the brothers as they stood
there trying to formulate their plan.

"Okay."

The alpha said to the others.

"Two of us are going to run ahead and make
our way to the truck. Charlie and I are the
fastest so we will run ahead. When we get to the
truck we will get it running then mow through
this field and grab you little brother."

"What the fuck?"

The smallest and injured brother said
pissed off his brothers would leave him alone at
all.

"Look god damn it if we don't get this truck going and fast we are all dead, you got that?"

The new alpha told his little brother.

"We sure as fuck can't get you to the damn hospital without the fucking truck."

The smaller of the medium sized brother said following his larger brothers lead.

"I am already going to have to nigger rig that fucking thing together just to get it to go and I am the best fucking mechanic out of the three of us. You want to get out of here or not?"

"Fine it's all on you, both you fuckers when I die."

The small injured brother cried.

"Fuck you man, that dude is gone by now."

The alpha told his little brother knowing he was lying.

"Yeah you already said that before remember?"

The injured brother called out.

"What did we find after this fucker was long gone? I don't know our brother with his fucking face cut off and part of his heart fucking eaten! Go to hell you dumb mother fuckers, what the hell type of shit do you think that we are dealing with here?"

The injured brother yelled as he slapped his larger brother across the face. At that moment the three brothers all began fighting,

the fear had taken them all. The medium size
brother tried to break up the fight.

"Look there is a crazy fucker out there
hunting us, probably watching us right now and
you two are fucking fighting? This shit is to
fucking real and I am getting the fuck out of
here."

He yelled at his two brothers.

"We are all fucked if we don't get as far
the fuck away from here as we can, and as fast
as we can. We fucked up, we so fucked up."

The smallest brother said crying holding
his broken leg.

"This shit hurts so fucking bad, I don't
even care anymore, I just want to get the fuck
out of here. Please Lord, please Lord let me

just get out of here alive. I promise to dedicate the rest of my life to you Lord. Dear Lord I beg you for forgiveness for all that I have done. I promise I will spend the rest of my life on my Knee's praying to you Lord."

The injured brother begged and pleaded to God, tears in his eyes.

The two brothers began to laugh at their little brothers pleas with the Lord. The larger of the brothers slapped his little brother on his back.

"I bet you would love being on your knee's for the rest of your life."

The three brothers all began laughing, I almost laughed myself thinking with my Beavis and Butt-Head mind.

"Fuck you assholes!"

The injured brother said laughing. I had to laugh I would probably have picked on my brother as well had he said some gay ass shit like the injured brother had.

Poor fool for actually thinking that God or the Gods actually worked that way. I truly hate that shit. What the fuck do people think, that you can do some fucked up ass shit, you can rape, you can kill, you can torture, and there will be no repercussions for your actions? Fucking bullshit, you made your decisions, you chose to do each and everything that you have done, good, bad, fucking evil you chose to do each action. I have killed more people than I can count, I have raped, I have tortured, every manor of evil I have fucking done. I well I own every one of my actions, not owning ones actions is simple weakness in my eyes. Just hearing this bitch of a man say all of that shit while crying honestly made me taste a bit of vomit in my mouth.

"Fuck this we are going to get the truck."

The alpha told his brothers. I could see the terror on the injured brother's face. The smaller of the medium sized brother didn't look to be doing so well himself. Fear, fear is a sickness polluting the body, in the case of these brothers, the injured brother looked as if his fear had him at stage four cancer. The other two brothers were scared, yet I would put them at a stage three cancer. Even I am scared, scared to die myself, all I know is that I want to do is die like a warrior. Old age was never promised to me, in fact I highly doubt that I will ever see old age. One day my number will come up, in a weird way I am excited for the day.

The two brothers took off in a dead run, their injured brother between the two of them towards the cabin. I give them no more than a full two minuet's and I was sure that they would be totally out of breath and would have to stop. Hell the running was hard as fuck for me and while not in great shape, I at least have muscle memory. Not to mention that these guys are both carrying half of the weight of their brother. I was happy that they decided not to leave him as a sacrifice in the end, a little more of a pain in my ass, yet valiant none the same. These fuckers had no way to make the full run, even if fueled by fear. I expected that their lungs must be on fire by now. My hope was that they would make it to the halfway point before they stopped. I estimate that this is around a half a mile distance.

"Come on man, just try and help."

The larger of the brother said to his injured brother's arm wrapped around his shoulder.

"Just help man, we need to get to the truck as fast as we can."

"I'm fucking trying to my leg hurts so fucking bad."

Personally I hate weakness, only in this day and age does weakness survive hell thrive. Only till recently only the strong survived, as it should be.

"Come on man."

The smaller of the medium sized brothers
said.

"I'm trying, I'm fucking trying."

The injured brother cried out if
frustration. I was only five feet from them at
most, moving with the shadows.

"Stop, please stop, just for a second."

The injured brother cried.

"My leg, my leg feels like it is going to
explode."

As the brothers stopped the larger of the
brothers walked ahead maybe ten to fifteen feet.
I am only steps away from him. I can smell his
sweat, damn near taste the salt from his body in
the air.

I wanted the injured brother to know that he was dying. I know that I have to take out the larger brother first now they didn't leave the little guy behind, yet I wanted to have some fun with him as well. I lay in the shadows for just from the two brothers that had stayed behind, waiting for my moment like a tiger getting ready to attack. I am just two feet away from the larger of the two brothers, hidden by the shadows. The larger brother just turned his back to me. I leaped from my hiding spot deep within the shadows with the handle of my blade I smash him in the side of his head, knocking him out cold. He falls to the ground, I quickly grab him and smash my blade down into his leg cutting his Achilles tendons in both legs. The tendons are tough as I cut them. The larger of the brother's blood pours from his legs on to the earth.

"What falls to the ground is the Lords."

I whisper in his ear.

"Let the earth drink her fill."

The whole encounter took mere seconds, I
pounced upon the little injured brother. With a
swift kick I smashed him in the side of his face
with my foot breaking his jaw. He was trying to
scream but only grunts came out of his mouth now
that his jaw was no longer functional. I looked
down at his jaw literally hanging off of his
face and smiled.

"What's up little man?"

I asked poking at his jaw?

"You know I heard every word of that gay
ass shit that was pouring out of your mouth back
there. I don't blame your brothers for picking

on you, they wanted to leave you, a sacrifice if you will. Why do you think that they wanted to leave you? Let me tell you boy, you are the weakest link, they knew I was out here just like you did."

I laughed still poking at his hanging jaw.

"Do you really think that God will forgive you?

I am serious boy, do you really think that God will forgive you, do you really believe that bullshit?"

I actually wanted to hear this little bitches answer.

"Please don't kill me, please don't kill me. I am sorry, I am so, so sorry."

He cried barely intelligible.

"Yes, please I will give my life to God, just please don't kill me."

"Well boy your life will be given to god believe that. Although I do not believe that it will go the way in which you had hoped for. You see boy, I have no clue whatever God it is that you pray to will forgive you for all of the evil ass shit that you have done, personally I don't care if he does. My mission is to get you to him so that you can ask him for that forgiveness you so long for."

I said as I poked him in the cheek with my blade. I laughed as blood poured from his cheek mixed with tears.

"You are no better than me, no better than us you fucking bastard."

"Really, shit boy I never said that I was. The difference between you and I is that I hold no images of grandeur in my heart and soul, I know that I am better than no man. As well boy unlike you I have never felt the desire to ask the Gods to forgive me for any of my actions. Unlike you boy I am a man, I own my decisions, good or bad they are my own. I have no fear of hell, nor do I care about heaven, nor God for that damn matter. You see God made me exactly how I was supposed to be. Now get on your knee's boy.

I want you to pray, pray to your God and see if he answers you."

I ordered my head facing the sky as if I were looking for the Heavenly Father himself.

"Pray boy, pray boy, now ask for your goddamn forgiveness."

I grabbed him by his shirt and pulled it from him.

"I said pray boy, fucking pray. Your time is so very near, you better let your God know that you are coming to him."

"Please oh Lord in heaven forgive me my sins. Forgive me for all of the evil that I have done, I beg of you."

I knelled down beside the injured brother.

"Do you think he heard you? More so, do you think that he actually cared at all?"

I asked slapping him softly against his broken jaw.

"How many of your victims begged you for forgiveness, how many of them cried out to God asking for his help before you raped, tortured, and killed them? My son I am Gods messenger, I have been sent here by God himself to clean up his fuck ups, and you and your fucked up family are one of those fuck ups.

Well fucker I hope for your sake that your God was listening and heard you well through that fucked up jaw of yours. If you are lucky just maybe you will be forgiven. Hell kid maybe we will all get lucky and each be forgiven of all of our sins, but to be real with you, I doubt it. As I see it though man, if your God cared about you then you wouldn't be here with me. I hope for your sake that your God does forgive you, but sadly for you, I don't forgive."

With that I ran my blade across his throat cutting all the way down to the spine. I pulled the head back exposing the spinal column a bit. I pushed my knife between the cracks and cut through the cartilage severing the head from the body.

I then took my blade and carved a cross into the injured brother's chest. I then carved a message for the others, God does not forgive, nor do I. I left the body on its knees, the head in front of it, the face looking up towards the heavens. Lastly I carved evil in big letters across the dead brother's forehead.

"Chapter 15"

I could see that the other brother was starting to stir now. In all of my fun I had almost forgotten about him. I pounced upon him and began to cut his clothes from his body with my knife. I quickly shoved part of his shirt into his mouth and tied the rest around his head so that he couldn't scream. I then smashed my fist down into his nose breaking it. While I enjoyed doing this I had other motives, my main goal was to blind and disorient the brother for a while.

He was trying to fight me but I could tell whatever true strength that he had left was long ago spent. It seems that this poor fool just didn't have the stamina that one would need for a day such as today, I am surprised that I do.

"Save that energy there baby cakes. You are going to need it to crawl to your freedom."

The poor fool not realizing that I had cut his Achilles tendons tried to stand up only to fall directly to the ground. I broke out laughing.

"Oh about that sorry baby cakes you will never be on the dance floor again. Sorry man, no mambo number five or that horrible hillbilly line dancing shit you most likely do.

You my friend are a message to your other brother."

The brother was trying to get his bearings then he saw his younger brother's head sitting in front of him. At that moment he began to writhe and twist, turning his body like a worm.

I couldn't help but laugh at his attempts all of which simply led to more frustration.

"Sorry baby cakes you are not getting out of here on those feet. Yet I am going to be nice and let you test your strength and crawl out of here. I figured it out earlier it's only a little over a mile till you get back to the lane. Look, it's straight ahead of you, straight down this very row, your freedom, can you taste it can't you cup cake? I am sorry but I can't allow this to be easy for you at all. On the real man, I don't think you can make it to freedom, I just don't think that you have it in you."

I said as I placed my hand on his head pushing his face into the dirt.

"You see man I need to make this a bit more challenging for you. I want you to think about all of your victims that thought or tried to get away. All of those victims that had to crawl, hoping, dreaming, praying they would make their way to freedom. How many were there? Do you even remember, do you remember how many people you kidnapped, raped, tortured, killed, and then cannibalized? Shit I myself have killed hundreds of people. I will say though I never thought I would meet some real Texas Chainsaw Massacre type mother fuckers here in fucking North East Nebraska. This shit is just beyond fucked up to me man. You know Baby cakes I heard that movie was based on a real story, but damn you never believe that shit like that or families like that actually exist. I say this believing that fuckers like you really never could exist, boy was I wrong.

I mean for real, we all know that there are serial killers out there but whole families of them. Fuck man your whole family is like Jeffery Dhamer meets fucking Deliverance. For real man it is enough to blow a person's fucking mind."

I laughed astonished at my own disbelief.

"I am seriously having a hard time wrapping my head around the concept that a family like yours actually exist. Hell I cheered for the fuckers in that movie The House of a Thousand Corpses, but had I knew people like that actually existed I would have changed my tune. Maybe I just wanted to fuck that hot blonde in the movie like everyone else. Still that was a movie and the reality that people like you

actually exist is fucking mind blowing. As I see
it buddy for fuckers like you to exist God be
God a he or a she must have been sleeping while
you son's o bitches slid out of the lab and onto
the earth on your bellies before God woke up."

It dawned on me that many may consider me a
fucked off killer, a serial killer with a
paycheck. Yes I had killed in the name of my
country but that didn't mean that I didn't get
enjoyment out of doing so. What I did I did in
part for the country that I love, the country
that I swore to serve and protect. The other
part, well the other part I did for the joy I
got out of killing. I remember one day back in
Iraq, I took out over fifty insurgents in that
one damn day. They were like picking off prairie
dogs back in Nebraska to me. Another sniper on
the same point as I was took down thirty five.

We were communicating back and forth on or coms, taking bets on who could kill the most. We even had a bet for who could get the most head shots, body shots, you name it we bet on it. So yeah, some would say I may be a bit fucked up, yes I did enjoy my work, but I did it all for you, to protect you America.

"Well there buddy, it's time to get all of this shit started right. How many of your victims were in this exact situation as you right now cup cake? Look at you naked, bleeding, scared, alone, you are terrified I can tell, afraid death could come for you at any moment, so were they."

I said this as I slapped old boy on his ass.

"I am giving you a gift man, I am letting you know, letting you feel your victim's pain and frustration, you will know what they felt now, for however long you live, we will see about that one. I pulled out my blade, look at this blade cup cake, this blade has killed all of your brothers, and it will kill you and your other brother soon enough. Look at this blade, this is the same blade that gutted my friend Jill, that was her name, Jill. I like this blade, I am going to keep it as a war prize, keeps a good edge to. You guys get this from working in the packing house up in Norfolk? My old man used to work there, I knew I had seen a blade like this before. Not a good thing that this edge is so damn sharp for you."

"Please, please, I will never kill again I promise you, I will vanish man, just let me live."

"What the hell is up with you fuckers always begging for your lives? For real, do you really think after all you have seen me do that I am going to show you mercy at all? I mean for fucking real?"

I laughed looking at the crying, naked man lying on the ground before me.

"Did you ever show mercy to any of your victim's? Did you show my friend Jill any mercy when you were raping her? No, no you didn't, you showed zero mercy, so why would I?

You know what you have given me an idea you son of a bitch. I want you to understand true fear before you die, pain, well while fun seems like I am just not using enough imagination. I want you to know what it feels like to know death before it ever embraces your bitch ass."

I rolled the poor naked pathetic hillbilly onto his back.

"Here we go cup cake, enjoy this."

With that I pushed my blade into his belly opening it up to the fading light of the sun.

"You see these boy, these are your innards, not so pretty huh?"

I pulled the brothers entrails from his body laying them on the ground in front of him.

"How does this feel, do you like seeing your insides?"

The brother let out the loudest scream that I had ever heard in my life.

"There you go boy, let it all out, let your other brother know death is coming for him as well. Let that fear flow throughout your entire body, feels sickening doesn't it?"

I took my blade and opened cupcakes leg exposing the artery. Rather than simply sever it which would let him bleed out in two or three minuet's I made a small cut. This ensured his death but prolonged it by a good ten minuet's.

"Scream cupcake scream, let the world know where you are, who knows maybe your brother will save you, maybe you will live through all of this after all?"

I took my hand and smeared it into cupcakes blood.

"Look at me boy, remember me when you die."

I licked the blood on my hand getting a decent size mouth full of it. I then covered my face with his blood. Cupcake began screaming again.

"Scream boy, scream, its music to my fucking ears. Well it's time for me to go, you know that you can crawl to your freedom, to your brother. Look right down this row is your freedom, isn't that what you want?"

With that I made my way back into the field, only one left I thought.

"Chapter 16"

Cupcake as I was now calling him was screaming at the top of his exposed lungs. To be honest I was surprised that he had so much left in him. Yet I could hear each of his screams getting a bit weaker each time that he called out. His time was nearing, soon he would be able to sit in front of his creator, hell, whatever comes next, it is there that he can explain his actions. You see that is what we are truly judged on, what we chose to do with the gift that God gave us, the gift of life. That does not mean that some people are not simply born bad people. No, now and again a few slip through the cracks and some simply sick fucks are allowed to live on earth. Maybe they are allowed to live so that we can know good and evil, to see who will stand up and protect the flock when in the face of true evil. Maybe like I said earlier God was just sleeping or to damn busy and they were able to slip through, who knows.

No God gives us the gift of free will, we have the ability to choose. That is why the angels hated us, angels were made to serve they were not blessed with free will like us. I don't blame the Devil for being all pissed off about that one. We have the ability whether we want to decide to worship or not, it's all up to us. Faith, faith is very hard for even the best of us. I will admit that all that I have ever truly had faith in is my own desire to live and my gun. I have let myself down a few times, but my gun, she has always been true to me. Faith is a so called God, shit most of us can't find any resemblance of faith in ourselves, how the fuck are we supposed to have faith in God.

Not only do we get to decide whether or not we believe or not, we have the ability to decide our own actions. Now I am no Hindu nor am I a

Buddhist, so I will not even begin to try and understand the laws of Karma. Yet as I look at it Karma makes a lot of sense. We choose to be just people, good people, all working for the betterment of all mankind. On the flip side we choose if we will be a killer, a rapist, or even cannibals like this sick ass group of albums. You can also choose the route that I took, I killed hundreds of people. I have always said that I do what I do for a cause, something greater than myself. I have always said that I have done what I have to protect America, to protect freedom. Yet I find myself asking what has killing any towel head in the mountains of Afghanistan really do to protect America or her citizens? The reality is half of these fuckers most likely were barely living outside of the damn Stone Age. I never protected anyone in the end, I knew it even then, just as I do now. No, I enjoyed it, I volunteered for every mission I took. I simply did what I did because I enjoyed it. I was just afraid to admit it to myself back then is all.

If I was supposed to have chosen a different path, well it is far too late for that now. In a different dimension I sell insurance or some other lame ass shit. I have a cute little family, two cars, a mortgage, the whole deal, the American dream right? I do believe now that we are given multiple paths that we can take. Each of these paths can and will take us to a different life path, a totally different existence, a different you.

The truth is we rarely see these paths or even begin to understand them till years later, long after they have passed. It is what it is I guess, es la vida, Que no? These bastards had all begged for their lives, telling me that they would all change, take a different path. I will never change my ways, nor will I beg for my life. As I see it I am perfect, made exactly how the Gods wanted me to be. I had the ability to travel different paths, I just didn't. I am sure that these fuckers had the exact same ability to do so as well. Just like me they could have gone and become lawyers, or even doctors. They chose to me killers, just like I did. You want to know something, killing people is easy. All it takes to kill a man is that first time. Right then you learn if you can be a killer or not. Do you know what I learned, they only thing that I learned the first time that I killed a man? I learned

that not only could I kill a man, I could do it
again.

That is the key, can you kill again? With
each kill it just gets easier and easier, you
pretty much separate yourself from the actual
act of killing. It's almost not even real
anymore with all of the technology, it's as if
when you are looking through your scope you are
looking at a video game. The true test is the
first person that you kill with a blade. Now a
blade, a blade makes it real you are up close
and personal. You feel your victim's heartbeat,
you smell their sweat, taste their fear. When
you cut a man or a woman's throat you can taste
the minerals in their blood in the air. That's
right you can taste their death in the air, now
that is a kill. After my first kill with a blade
I not only learned that I could do it again, I

learned that I loved it, I loved the rush of it,
and it became my drug.

"Chapter 17"

I quickly made my way towards the cabin to
dispose of the last brother. I was moving fast
but low as to not make the corn stalks move at
all. I could hear cupcake still yelling off in
the distance. I could see the last brother
looking out as he tried to fix the truck as fast
as he could. He was trying to fix the gas lines,
I should have just blown the fucker up when I
had the chance. No, that would have brought out
the fire department I am sure, its better that I
didn't do it that way. This is Nebraska, if a
farmer see's some smoke he always comes to

investigate. Not so much that he was worried or alarmed but more so for an excuse to stop and shoot the shit. That is just the way of the Nebraska farmer for better or worse. In all honesty they can be a bit nosy in my opinion, but hey this is their land, their home.

I couldn't believe that this bastard wasn't even going to try and help his brother. I didn't get how he could sit there and listen to his brothers screams and not try and help him. The only thing that this fucker cared about was saving his own ass. I am a military man at heart, I joined at seventeen, left two days after I graduated high school for boot camp. It was the military that taught me to be a real man. The military taught me the value of the team, no I in team. You see that is what boot camp is really about, making you a part of a team. We all went in as individual boys, each one with his own ego. Boot camp knocks you down, boot camp stomps that ego into the dirt, that entire sense of individualism. We all became part of a team, hell an elite team at that. I not only learned that you never leave a man behind, you know that you would be willing to risk your own life to do so. These men, these fellow soldiers are not even your blood, imagine what I would be willing to do for my own blood. This son of a bitch didn't even care about his own brother's screams. As I see it, it is my duty to be my brother's keeper.

I watched the last of the brother's peak out from under the truck and quickly make his way back under it again. I could hear him swearing to himself about the whole situation, calling his brothers idiots. Better them than me

I kept hearing him say, stupid fuckers getting

themselves killed, fuck them, he kept repeating.

I could tell this was his real reason for

ditching his brothers, let me get them so he

could have time to make his escape. What a bitch

of a man, does anyone have any bravery left in

them anymore, I asked myself? I blame the damn

TV, hell our very culture these days. By

eighteen I was already in some god awful shit

hole not only being shot at, but having to

return fire as well. Kids these days say that

they need a damn safe place. A safe room where

no one can harm them with words, fucking

pussies. Do you know what the enemy's safe place

is? The enemy has no safe places, the enemy

knows that any moment may be their last. The

enemy is not afraid of blood, not afraid of

bombs, yet our youth are afraid of being hurt by

words. I am afraid that we have already doomed ourselves.

I moved in silence, the last of the brothers didn't even begin to notice me. I am a tiger, creeping out from the edge of the jungle. I could see the brother's feet hanging out from under the truck. I moved in closer and closer till I was only feet from my next victim. I could hear him still swearing, saying how the hell he was going to get out of there and fuck everyone else. Weakness, I hate nothing more than weakness. I looked up to the heavens, God if you are up there thank you for this, I said in a silent prayer.

I made my move, I grabbed the brother's feet and drug him out from under the truck. He instantly began to fight me as I expected him to do so. I slammed down on top of him smashing my blade into his belly. Anything in the gut is always horribly painful. Not only do you know death is coming when you get stabbed or shot in the gut, but you get to feel each and every second of it. On top of the last brother holding him down with my weight I twisted my blade inside of him. I pulled my blade from his belly and quickly cut his Achilles tendons.

"Sorry my friend I can't have you trying to run away on me."

I picked up the brothers face that I had cut off earlier from the ground.

"What the hell is this man, no love or respect for your brother?"

I looked down on the final living brother and looked at the severed face of the other.

"Damn you two inbred fucks really do look a lot alike. Here let me check something out sunshine."

I laughed as I placed the severed face over the living brothers.

"Wow, what a great fit man, seems you guys shared the same bone structure as well."

The final brother began crying and begging as his brothers had before him.

"Please, please, please don't kill me."

"Don't kill you, you stupid hillbilly fuck are you so damn inbred that you can't realize that I have already killed you? Honestly, do you actually think that you will survive that belly wound man? You know when I twisted my blade, the same one that killed your other brothers I cut open your stomach, emptying all of that acid all over your innards. Not only that but I cut into your bowels, you will be septic in an hour and die man whether I finish you off or not, and badly mind you.

I didn't allow any of your other brothers to live, why would I let you live man, come on. To be honest I am so damn sick of all of this begging from you guys. Each of you has begged for their life before I killed them, have some respect and man up, accept your death. Please, please, please don't kill me out of each of your mouths."

I stood over the final brother's face.

"Please, please, please. Nope, don't work does it, fucking bitch."

"I'm sorry about the girl, I am fucking sorry man."

"Yeah, me to, Jill was her name. Don't be sorry though man, Jill died for a cause. Jill died so that we would come together and I could kill you all. I do feel like this may just be some biblical type shit. As I see it you sick fucks slipped through the cracks. God sent me to you to fix up one of his mistakes he made. Fuck man I am like a Knights Templar right now."

"You are just a crazy person who got the drop on us. God did not send you God would want you to show mercy."

"Maybe, maybe God would want me to show you mercy, sadly for you I am not God I show no mercy. Enough talk, for fucks sake I am sick of you idiots constant begging."

With that I grabbed the brother's jaw and forced it open. I pulled out the brother's tongue as far from his mouth that I could and began slicing through it with my blade. I began to fill the brother's bloody mouth with dirt. The idiot was coughing blood and dirt, covering himself in a muddy mess.

"You here that sunshine, no more goddamn begging. You remember raping my friend? I remember you raping her. You know now that you don't have a tongue in your mouth I think that you need something else in your mouth sunshine."

I pulled down the final brothers pants and grabbed his cock and balls. I began cutting, severing this son of a bitch's man hood free of his body. He tried to scream, yet with no tongue and mouth full of blood and mud he couldn't do so. I took his cock and balls and shoved them into his mouth pushing them all the way down his throat.

"There you go sunshine, you want to come at me with all that gay ass begging it seems only fitting that you die with a cock in your mouth."

I could see that he was fading out quickly, death was already taking him. The reality was that I am sure that he has already lost half of the blood in his body by now. I kind of regretted not making him really suffer more really, he deserved a far harsher death. If I would have had the time I would have captured and tortured all of them. Allowed each one to watch the other one die. I could have played a game that I used to play in the mountains of Afghanistan, choose who dies next.

I would let them decide who was going to die next, it is a real mind fuck of a game really. The group decides who dies next each hoping they will be let go, yet forced to watch each person die not knowing if they are next. What is best is that deep down they know they will get a turn being tortured to death, they are just prolonging what is sure to come. Yeah that game got one hell of a price put on my head. Word got out really quick about the evil American who worked for Satan. Even the brass caught word of that little game, like I said earlier, I always played dumb, deny, deny, and deny that is the rule. They didn't actually care at all, I got results and results are all that mattered. Deep down they knew that made me into the monster that I was, that I am today.

"Chapter 19"

I sat for the next ten minuet's watching the final brother die. His body was blue from the loss of blood. I enjoyed watching him die, I thought about cutting his throat, ending him quicker but I wanted to let him die slow, ponder just why it was he was dying. I sat there covered in blood, I had killed all of these bastards, sick fucks. The sun had fallen below the horizon finally, day had given way to light, a never ending battle. I felt as if I began to fall into a meditative state, I am one with everything, one with the universe.

I thought that I would feel happy after I killed these bastards. I thought that I would feel joy, elation, something anything at all.

Yet I feel nothing, as if none of this had really mattered. I like always am cold and uncaring. I am indifferent to the world.

I came to my senses if you will, it was time to clean up my, mess. I made my way first to the last kill by the truck. I grabbed the body and began to drag it towards the other bodies. I drug each body through the corn field, it was almost a bit spooky in the field in the darkness. The moon lit my way, as if I were a grave digger in some old Edgar Allen Poe book. I brought each of the bodies down to the shore of the creek. It took me close to an hour to get all of the bodies down to the water's edge but I was in no hurry. Getting the bodies to the water was the easy part, I simply let them roll down the embankment till they hit the bottom.

Once the bodies were all at the water's edge I opened each belly to allow the water to fill the body cavity and sink it to the bottom of the pool. With all of the silt and mud in this creek I didn't doubt that they wouldn't be covered in a matter of days. Between the mud, the catfish, the crawdads, the turtles, and every other critter in the creek these bodies would never be found. It is for the best, these fools deserved to simply vanish. Only Jill deserved more, it made me sad to know that I had to send her to the bottom of the creek with these bastards. No one would miss these sick fucks, but Jill, well at least I know that I will miss Jill.

I pushed each of the bodies into the pool. It was nice to watch them float for just a second, then slip below the dark water lit only by the moonlight. Brought me back to childhood, the body that I found at the bottom of the river. I placed the last brother into the creek. I hated them all, I am happy to have killed them. If given the chance I would kill them all again, only this time I would torture them even more. I took off all of my clothes and washed them in the creek. I then jumped in and cleaned off my own body. It felt good to wash the mud and dried blood from my body, as if I were being reborn to this world, baptized in the river like Jesus himself by John the Baptist. My clothes all clean I climbed the bank naked and made my way back into the tree to allow my clothes to dry and get some sleep if possible.

I closed my eyes and instantly fell asleep. It felt good to sleep, before I passed out I wasn't quite sure if I was back in Afghanistan or not. I know that I have been out of the military for far too long, I am too old to reenlist, I can go MERCK though.

I have a purpose again, I have said it before Jill didn't die in vain. Jill's death brought me back to reality, allowed me purpose again. I am a killer, I am a warrior. I woke up just before the sunrise. I got dressed and quickly fixed the gas lines to the truck. I drove south heading towards Kansas City. There is an office for Black Well there, Americas Mercenaries. I signed the dotted line, just like I had when I was seventeen. Two hours later I find myself on a plane. I have not been told where I was going, I don't even care. All I know is that it is sure to be someplace very bad, someplace no one else wants to go. I am off to a war zone. Finally once again I am on my way

home.

Often the greatest calm

exist within the chaos